"I can't explain my behavior toward you...

"I lose control of myself somehow," Peter said. "I don't understand it."

"I don't understand it, either." Of all the men to be attracted to, Mary Ellen had to go and get attracted to one who believed long-term commitment was a mistake of nature. "Maybe it really is Cupid at work. After all, I shot you in the butt on Valentine's Day. That's got to be significant."

"I wish I could blame such a thing as Cupid. But the only significance to your arrow shot is that you have bad aim."

"But I don't. That's the point."

"I got the point." He taped the doughnut ring under his rear end. "It wasn't from good aim."

She waved a hand. "How we met doesn't matter anymore. All I know is that it started something. We're attracted to each other. You call it a chemical imbalance. I call it a force of nature. Chemical imbalance or not, what are we going to do about it?"

Dear Reader,

You're about to meet the Holiday cousins—Peter, Michael, Raymond and Jared. They're four sexy guys with two things in common: the Holiday name and humbug in the heart! But this year, Cupid's working overtime and by Christmas he's aiming to have the Holiday cousins singing love songs!

Linda Cajio brings you the first book in THE HOLIDAY HEART miniseries. Here, Peter sees a new side to Valentine's Day. In the months ahead, follow the other cousins' stories set around Mother's Day, Labor Day and Christmas.

American Romance is delighted to welcome Linda Cajio, a name known to readers of romance fiction. She is the author of over twenty bestselling contemporary and historical romances, is a past president of Romance Writers of America and the winner of several writing awards. Linda makes her home in New Jersey, with her family.

Be sure you don't miss any of the Holiday men in THE HOLIDAY HEART series!

Regards,

Debra Matteucci
Senior Editor and Editorial Coordinator
Harlequin
300 E. 42nd St.
New York, NY 10017

Linda Cajio

DOCTOR VALENTINE

Harlequin Books

TORONTO • NEW YORK • LONDON
AMSTERDAM • PARIS • SYDNEY • HAMBURG
STOCKHOLM • ATHENS • TOKYO • MILAN
MADRID • WARSAW • BUDAPEST • AUCKLAND

Much thanks goes to Constance O'Day-Flannery and Colleen Quinn,
who have listened to my stories for years now and who keep listening
and advising. What a great writers' support group!

Thanks to my agent, Laura Blake of Curtis Brown, who has more
faith than I do at times. You're terrific. And thanks to my editor,
Denise O'Sullivan, who took a chance on *Doctor Valentine* and the
entire Holiday Heart miniseries, and is now bringing the books to life.

This book is for Jack, who always hangs in there. It's been twenty-five
years, babe. God love ya, because I do!

ISBN 0-373-16667-2

DOCTOR VALENTINE

Chapter One

"Romantic love is merely an imbalance of the brain's chemicals. If we could control them, imagine all the good we could do. There would be no more obsessive relationships. No more time wasted daydreaming. No more heartbreak and moping. Production would go up. People would lead normal lives. Calm would reign over man and woman."

Dr. Peter Holiday smiled broadly after making his declaration. The small group of men surrounding him nodded thoughtfully. All but one. Jeremy Chelios, rival for the Magnussen research grant, smirked.

Peter merely raised his eyebrows. He had left the confines of the Magnussen mansion, where afternoon tea was being held and had joined the cigar and pipe smokers out on the back lawn, knowing these men had influence with Philadelphia magnate John Magnussen. The enormous house had floor-to-ceiling terrace doors galore, yet no smoking was allowed inside the leather-and-mahogany surroundings. Magnussen preferred his guests to stroll outside among the formal topiaries and clipped boxwoods. Not that Peter minded where one could smoke. He didn't indulge. But to make his points, he'd go where the power brokers were. He had to.

No one would deter Peter from snagging the research grant for his behaviorial-study center and his special project of controlling emotional responses—the most promising being romantic love, which caused all kinds of problems. Especially not Jeremy Chelios, whose life work featured a poisonous Amazonian tree frog.

The sun shone brightly, warming the winter garden on this fourteenth of February. No time was more appropriate to sew up the grant than on Valentine's Day. Poetic justice. The upcoming symposium on the first of March, when the candidates would make their final presentations, would just be the icing on the cake.

"Think of it," Peter continued, wanting to stress his point with his colleagues. He intended to crush his opponent with his logic, to show that Chelios's work held little merit. "If we could control our emotional responses *before* they happen, we would have more control of our individual lives and therefore a less overwrought population. Love is a perfect example of how our emotions overrule common sense. It makes us forget everything when we're in the throes of it. We act like idiots. Our work suffers, our families suffer. We disturb our neighbors. We do crazy things, hurtful things. On the other hand, animals' unpredictable responses are based solely on moments of danger and survival, not emotions. Most of the time they live together quite compatibly. They don't experience love. People are the only beings who do. Eliminate romantic love and we would have a much better world. I guarantee it—"

The interruption came from behind him.

Peter heard a faint whirring sound, followed by a

thonk. An enormous pain erupted in his left buttock. He clutched himself, faintly surprised to feel something other than his clothing, skin and muscle at his nether regions. He looked over his shoulder.

An arrow was sticking out of the side of his butt.

"Oh, God," he muttered, sinking to his knees. His head spun wildly, and he thought he would pass out. He swallowed back bile, determined not to humiliate himself in front of these influential men.

"Call 911!" Jeremy shouted, rushing for the house.

Peter tried to disagree, not wanting to be beholden to Chelios of all people. But the wound throbbed deeply, the muscle pulsing almost unbearably. Tears pushed at Peter's eyes. He couldn't speak.

"Omigosh!" A feminine voice seemed to float around Peter's head like a ring of chirping birdies— there and yet distant. He sensed bodies crowding around him. A worried face came into his view as a woman knelt in front of him. Rich, auburn hair curved around a narrow, lightly freckled face. Cornflower blue eyes stared at him while full, kissable lips moved. "I'm so sorry! The shot went wide. Are you all right?"

Although he had never met her, he knew who she was—her reputation for impulsiveness preceding her. This was Mary Ellen Magnussen, John's daughter. Instinct urged him to do something violent. Common sense warned him to stay cool with this woman. At least until her father made a decision on the grant. Oddly, his heart beat with what felt like anticipation. He was losing control and fast. "What do you think?" he said through tightly clenched teeth.

"There's no need to be testy." She paused. "Okay, so there is. Don't you want to lie down while we wait for the ambulance?"

He did. More than anything, he did. Stickiness seeped around his fingers, which still clutched his buttock. He glanced down, fascinated and repulsed at the polished wooden shaft and the green feather trim on its visible end. The other end lay buried in his flesh. *His flesh.* Logical thinking faded further from his brain.

"The Indians would yank the arrow out," Mary Ellen commented. "We could do that while we wait."

"Are you nuts?" Peter yelped, horrified by the thought of anyone pulling anything through his butt. Certain body parts should be sacred, his rear end being one of them. Besides, he had heard Mary Ellen had a penchant for doing the unexpected, sometimes even the unacceptable. Certainly anyone who eschewed a sedate tea for archery in February, no matter how mild the day, meant trouble. She wouldn't be pulling anything out of him if he could help it.

Mary Ellen wrinkled her nose at him. "No. I'm not nuts. You'd probably feel better once the arrow's removed. You'll have less risk of blood poisoning with it out. We only have to break the shaft—"

"Don't touch my shaft!" Peter gulped in more air. His brain was short on oxygen. "I'll wait for the professionals, thank you."

"It's bleeding worse," someone said.

"It is?" Peter gasped, in a panic.

Mary Ellen glanced around with him this time. Blood flowed freely now. When Peter's gaze returned to hers, she looked stricken and a little green. Not as green as he felt, however.

"If you plan to toss your cookies, do so in the house," he advised her. "I couldn't take that, too."

Her jaw squared. "I don't intend to. Lie down. We need to get a compress on it."

"No, thanks. I don't trust you to not try some make-shift surgery."

"Stop being a baby."

She pulled him forward, and never had he felt more like a baby when he couldn't stop her from laying him flat out on his stomach. Pain shot through him like a second arrow. But not enough for him to miss the fact that his face was positioned right between her knees.

"That's better," she said, shifting to his side.

"Little do you know," he muttered into the cold grass. His brain finally recognized the cause of his current problem. "You shot me!"

"Yes, I did. It was an accident." She jerked at the trouser cloth around his wound.

"Watch it!" Peter screeched, half turning toward her. He collapsed back from the pain.

"Sorry, but I can't take your pants off the normal way."

"Why would you want to take my pants off at all?"

"To staunch the wound, silly. But I have to see it first."

He heard cloth rip. Cool air swirled across his backside. Peter realized she had suited action to words and somehow exposed his wounded area. His buttocks were hanging out for all to see. He bet this had never happened to Freud. He bet Freud would have had a lot to say about *exposure gluteal*, too.

"Fascinating," one of the men with them said.

"Yes," another agreed. "Look at the way the muscle has closed around the opening, trying to seal it off."

A third put in his opinion. "No, no! It's trying to expel the foreign object."

Another voice objected. "You're both wrong. The body is simply accepting the arrow. Nothing more."

The men's discussion heated up at about the same rate as Peter's face. He gritted his teeth to keep from fainting or yelling. Calmly, he said, "Gentlemen, could we debate my fundament at another time, please?"

The group grew silent. Peter sighed in relief.

"Well, whatever it's doing, it looks good," Mary Ellen said cheerfully. "You must work out."

He frowned. "Why would you say that?"

"Nice muscle tone."

He had no clue whether to say thanks or not. Courtesy won out. "Thank you."

"You're welcome."

She pressed a cloth pad against his side, to staunch the bleeding. Her fingers touched his bare skin. A shiver ran up his spine. A hotter, more intense throbbing occurred lower down. Peter pressed his face into the grass. Why did he have this odd rush of emotions, as if he was almost exhilarated rather than wounded? Did one feel good when shot? It could be another area of emotion that needed exploring, because if this reaction were genuine, then it was nuts.

"Does it hurt?" Mary Ellen asked, leaning back on her heels.

"God, yes." He tilted his head and said louder, "Yes, it hurts. Why would you even ask?"

"I don't know. Curiosity."

She sounded indulgent. He hated indulgence. "Where the hell's the ambulance? I could walk at this rate."

"We could pull it out ourselves," she offered again.

The others murmured excitedly at her suggestion. Just what he needed—eagerness.

"You really like that thought, don't you?"

"I suppose it appeals to me to finish the job I started." She bent lower, managing to bring her lower body close up and personal. Her derriere was inches from his eyes. Her jeans pulled tight across her unblemished curves. He could easily imagine his hands coursing over her skin…soft skin like satin, skin holding her warmth—

"The ambulance should be here any moment."

Jeremy's voice shattered Peter's vision, both imagined and real. Mary Ellen shifted out of his range. He must be hallucinating with the pain.

"How are you feeling, Peter?" Jeremy sounded smug. Peter bet he *was* smug.

"I'm fine," Peter lied, trying to put strength in his voice. The effort sounded lame to his own ears.

"Don't be so macho," Mary Ellen said.

"Peter would bluster in an atomic blast," Jeremy told her. "No one pays attention."

Peter bit back a retort. It made no sense to argue when he was on the ground with an arrow in his butt.

"What's all this?"

The new voice sent Peter to his final humiliation. Of course, John Magnussen was bound to investigate the ruckus interrupting his stuffy tea for the research candidates. President of three corporations, board member of many more, yet with his heart in academia, Magnussen held the fate of many research projects in his hands. His own research desperate for funding, Peter knew this was not the moment to be seen with his pants down and an arrow in the most unusual of places. He was single-handedly shattering science's dignified facade, not to mention his own.

"It's my fault, Dad," Mary Ellen said. "My shot

went wide, a little too wide and I hit... What's your full name, Peter?''

"Peter Holiday," everyone said.

"Pleased to meet you, Peter Holiday," she said. To her father, she added, "I shot him. A total accident. I have no idea how the arrow got over here. It was as if a hand guided it—"

"Please, Mary Ellen," her father interrupted. "I'm having trouble buying that, so don't even begin to sell it to me."

"But Dad!"

"No. Just be quiet and keep your hand on Peter's ass."

"Dad!"

Peter flushed. Thirty-four years old and he was blushing because a woman had her hand on his rear with her father's permission. The father's approval caused the blush and he knew it.

"On the compress, dammit!" Magnussen corrected. "Where's that flipping ambulance?"

Peter waited in a haze, not wanting to witness his own further humiliation. Better to be half out of it, he thought.

At last the emergency paramedics arrived, flitting between the onlookers while whistling in awe and giggling with malice. Their hands were gentle, though, efficiently getting Peter onto a stretcher without causing more than minimal pain. The intravenous they had started probably helped.

Peter's last sight, before they closed the ambulance doors, was of Mary Ellen Magnussen staring back at him. For one moment, everything about her radiated an aura that reached into his soul. He had never been shot by a lovelier disaster.

Simple chemical imbalance seemed as logical as birds flying upside down and backward.

MARY ELLEN MAGNUSSEN pushed open the door to the hospital room and peered inside.

To her surprise, her victim was not lying on his stomach. Instead he lay in a normal, reclining position. She wondered if that put more stress on the wound and hoped not. He wasn't screaming in pain, so she took that as a good sign. Still, no nurse was present, and he could be suffering quietly, in great agony.

Agony she had caused him.

She couldn't explain what had happened. Rather than attend a tea for brainy scientists, she'd decided some archery practice was in order. No novice to the sport, she had almost made the Olympic team while in college. She thought she had clutched the arrow properly, but it took flight on its own. Literally. She had no excuse for such carelessness.

The mark it had found still amazed her. Peter Holiday. Brilliant, eccentric, gorgeous. The moment she had looked at him, she'd been intrigued. Maybe his helpless gaze, overlaid by brave words, had tugged at her heart. Maybe she'd just responded to the situation.

He had a nice tush, though, even with an arrow sticking out of it.

She gripped the bouquet she'd brought more tightly and opened the door wider. He turned to her, his ice blue eyes a striking contrast to his dark hair and olive skin. Women would find him handsome. With his craggy, virile features, he looked more like a football player than a behavioral scientist.

Mary Ellen paused, feeling captured and raked over the coals at the same time. The sensation caused an odd swirl of anticipation deep inside her. She forced it away and walked toward him. "Hi. How are you feeling?"

"Not much. They've pumped me full of pain-killers."

An awkward silence ensued. She coughed. "I thought I would come to see how you're doing."

"Why? Did you want to finish the job?"

"I'm really sorry about what happened, but there's no need to be nasty," she said. "If it's any consolation, I was questioned by the police for two hours. It seems they do that even with accidents."

Peter smiled. It lit his face, giving him an almost innocent, boyish look. Mary Ellen caught her breath, then let it out again. "You don't have to look so happy. They didn't arrest me," she said.

"Too bad."

She made a face and changed the subject. "How long will you be in here?"

"Overnight, I think. I'm the comic relief today."

She bet he was. She focused on his water pitcher, then lifted it and flipped open the lid. "Ice water. That's no good."

She went over to the sink and dumped out the contents.

"What are you doing?" he asked.

"Making you an arrangement." She poured warmer water into the temporary vase and went back to his portable table. She took an aspirin out of her purse and dropped it into the pitcher.

"Does the pitcher have a headache?"

"It's for the flowers. Keeps them fresh." She stuck the foot-long stems into the water. The moment she let go, the pitcher began to tip. She caught it before it landed on Peter. "One accident a day is enough."

"I'll say. By the way, what do I drink out of?" he asked.

She paused in rearranging the flowers. "I haven't a clue. I suppose you could ask for another jug."

"I suppose."

She set the vase on the table again and carefully let go. It stayed upright, the out-of-season daisies and carnations standing tall. She grinned. "Victory."

Peter eyed the arrangement dubiously. "One hopes."

"Pessimist." Curious, she bent down and peered at the side of the bed.

"What are you doing?"

"I wondered how you're sitting there. Doesn't it hurt?"

"For the moment, no. They've given me an inflatable ring to sit on, so at least I *can* sit. I'll probably have to use it for several weeks."

"Really?" She lifted the sheet to see the ring.

He slapped the coverings down. "I've been enough of a peep show, thank you very much."

She straightened. "I'm not looking for a peep, believe me."

"You had my pants off fast enough to admire your work."

"I wanted to stop the bleeding, nothing more. You are a grumpy one, aren't you?"

"Do you have any idea what you've done?" he asked. "My research is being reviewed by the Magnussen Foundation and that tea was an important step in the process. All the people who will influence the final decision were there. All the competitors for the grant were there. My reputation has to be sterling. My behavior has to be aboveboard. And you shot me in the...in the—"

"Butt?" Mary Ellen supplied helpfully.

"Butt. Have you any notion of how I looked, lying on the ground with an arrow in my behind?"

"Well, yes. I was there. I'll admit you looked a little silly—"

"Don't help me." He glared at her. "I could not afford to look silly on today of all days. I needed to look strong and dignified, like a man with a vision."

"You were a vision, all right."

"No thanks to you."

"Look. It was an accident! I can't explain what happened, but I'm truly sorry." She glared at him. "You're making more of this than you need to. I know the men on that committee. They'll make their recommendations to my father solely on the merits of the project. Nothing more. Tell me about your project and I'll tell you whether or not you've got a chance." She smiled. "I'll even help you. I know what they respond to, so I can tell you the best approach."

The anger left his face. "Really?"

"Sure. It's the least I can do to make up for what happened."

"Okay. I'm working on controlling emotional responses to outside stimuli, and I've had a breakthrough in one area. Have you ever experienced true romantic love?"

She blinked. "I beg your pardon?"

"True love," he repeated. "Not maternal or paternal love. Not sibling love or affection. I'm talking passionate love. Love that makes you crazy, insane, with all those highs and lows that keep you from being a

productive human being. The kind of love that breaks
you when it's over, that takes months and years to get
past—if you ever do. Have you experienced that?"

"Well..." she began, thinking back on her love life,
which looked mildly pathetic next to his description of
true love. She had been in love, even engaged once,
but never had she loved with the intensity that he
outlined.

"I believe...no, I have evidence that it is caused by
a chemical imbalance of the brain. And if so, it can be
controlled ...."

She listened, appalled, as he outlined his ideas and
research into that dreaded disease, love. He waxed enthusiastic on how it was a mating urge gone bad, punctuating each point by ticking it off on his fingers. He
finally wound down, leaving silence in the room.

Mary Ellen cleared her throat. "Have you ever considered the merits of weaving baskets for a living?"

He gaped at her. "What?"

"Mister, you're nuts! Passionate love separates us
from the animals, making us unique. Passionate love
inspires art and literature. Passionate love gives humans a joie de vivre no other emotion can give. Take
that away and we become zombies, just going through
life."

"Art and literature are inspired by more than passionate love," he countered. "Much more. Think of
the destruction love has caused. Nations have warred
over it. People have killed others and themselves because of it. Think of the cost to humanity, not to mention to taxpayers, all in the name of love. We would
not be zombies without passionate love. We would be
sane, sensible people. By eliminating those emotional

frenzies, we would be able to reach the next level as a civilized race.''

"You were hurt by love," she guessed. "You didn't like the lack of control, the vulnerability."

"Not me." He smiled smugly. "I am a scientist of human behavior. I observe."

"You're a virgin?"

"Of course I'm not a virgin!" He looked so indignant that she hid a smile. "But I have been in control of my emotions and I am a better man for it."

"You sound like a deranged Spock. Mister as opposed to Doctor."

"I know it works. My own parents were friends, not passionate lovers, when they married. They have a calm, comfortable relationship and totally trust each other. They are in agreement in all things. They found such equanimity without help, but millions won't naturally control their emotions as my parents did."

"They sound a whole lot like zombies. No offense. Lots of people marry for friendship, but that doesn't justify eliminating romantic love." An imp rose up inside Mary Ellen. Peter had everything so wrong that she wanted to put him back on the right path. The urge overwhelmed her until she *had* to act upon it.

She leaned forward, bringing her face close to his. He didn't move. She let the odd, swirling emotions wash over her, like a promise. "What about the excitement love creates?" She brushed her lips against his cheek in the lightest of touches. "What about the incredible feeling of skin on skin, intimately bound together in a commitment so precious not even eternity can break it?" She touched his other cheek in a second butterfly kiss. "What about satisfaction so deep that it robs your breath and touches every fiber of your being forever?"

"It's overrated." His voice was hoarse and his breath caressed her cheek in turn, sending shivers of delight down her spine.

"You think so?"

She kissed him. His lips didn't move under hers, but she was undeterred. He presented a challenge she could not ignore. She plied his mouth with her own, letting the kiss happen spontaneously. She stroked his cheek with her palm, then threaded her fingers through his hair. Running her tongue across his lips, she quested and coaxed until his mouth finally shifted. She took advantage of it, pressing closer.

His hands gripped her shoulders. She thought he would push her away. Instead, he pulled her to him until her breasts were crushed against his chest. His tongue met hers, expertly rubbing until her head spun dizzily. Noise roared in her ears. Her blood thickened, pulsing through her veins...pooling deep inside her belly. Suddenly, she was out of control, vulnerable to him, the emotions exciting and frightening.

When she finally broke the kiss, she dredged up every ounce of command over her body. She rose and walked to the door, then turned around. "I believe I've made my point, Professor."

"It's only lust. And that's 'Doctor.'"

"You need a better diagnosis, Doctor."

She got out of the room. As soon as she was alone in the elevator, she leaned against the wall and sank to the floor, her legs no longer able to support her. If Peter Holiday was just an observer, then she was a monkey's aunt. Brother, but could he kiss!

She wondered how to stuff Pandora back into the

box, because the wild woman was out and flying around, wreaking havoc everywhere.

PETER PRESSED HIS HANDS against his face, trying to squeeze out the taste and touch of Mary Ellen Magnussen. He pulled his fingers down his face and opened his eyes. It didn't help. Heat still burned him. Images overwhelmed him. He wanted more and more of her. Observer, hell. He wanted to be the guinea pig to her experiment about a thousand more times.

That wouldn't be enough. Not even close.

The flowers she'd brought stood brightly on the table. Peter picked them out of the pitcher, then dashed its contents onto his head. Water ran down his face, splattering his hair, pillow and chest. The half-dissolved aspirin stuck to his forehead. He pulled it off and popped it in his mouth, ignoring its sour taste.

"Just what the doctor ordered," he muttered.

He wished he could believe it.

Chapter Two

Peter sat down gingerly, making sure the doughnut pillow was perfectly centered under his posterior.

Pain jolted him. He shifted and the pain settled to a dull throb, enabling him to get through this meal. He'd been out of the hospital only a few days and was hardly ready for the kind of grilling he expected at a lunch with John Magnussen and the other candidates for the grant. Magnussen certainly liked to put the competitors together at social functions, where they tried to outdo one another. Peter wondered if the man had a sadistic streak, because these events were torture.

"How's the wound?" Magnussen asked.

Peter smiled and let the thoughts go. "Better."

More fool him if he were to complain. The other men at the table smirked, Jeremy Chelios most of all. Damn, why did Peter have to look like an idiot next to Jeremy? With past government cutbacks, they all scrambled for funding now. Like lions feeding at a carcass, the strongest got the most. Magnussen was shrewd prey, however. Obviously, he assessed everyone at these meetings. Not coming sent worse signals than coming. If only the luncheon was elsewhere than the Striped Bass restaurant. Peter hated fish, which was all the elegant, trendy restaurant served.

Magnussen talked in generalities during the meal. Peter expected nothing else; the man would give no clue to where he leaned. As Peter fiddled with his cod salad, pushing aside the fish pieces and eating the greens, he remembered Mary Ellen's reaction to his research. Had she influenced her father already? Could she? Had she told her father about the kiss? Peter could still taste it. No kiss had affected him like that, not in his entire thirty-four years. His reaction had been due to lust, of course. Only lust, a chemical imbalance. Anything else was impossible.

He suddenly realized she was walking toward the table. An invisible punch landed in his solar plexus. For a moment, he thought he had conjured her up, an image only. The notion was scary. The "image" came closer and became more real.

She had the most sensuous walk of any woman he'd ever seen. Her hips swayed slightly with her strong stride. She held her shoulders back, yet in a natural posture that enhanced the curve of her breasts. Her head tilted a little, as if in question. And a smile hovered about her mouth. Lord, but was this the woman who'd speared him in the backside on Valentine's Day? Each time he met her, he saw a totally different facet of Mary Ellen Magnussen.

His two other meetings with her had been disasters. Even the thought of a third was really scary. Peter braced himself.

"Hi, Dad," she said, sounding perfectly normal and reasonable. Peter knew better. "Gentlemen. How's the tush, Peter?"

"Surviving, thank you." He refused to allow the

urge to kill to show. Instead, he gripped his napkin under the table in a stranglehold.

"Take my chair, Mary Ellen," Jeremy volunteered, gallantly rising. "I'll have the waiter bring another."

"That's lovely of you," she said. "But I'm with several clients today. I just took a few moments to say hello."

Jeremy pulled his chair out farther. "Take my seat while you're here. I insist."

"Thank you." She smiled at him, then slipped into his seat. Jeremy pushed it forward, to leave more space in the aisle, then rested his hands on the chair back in a proprietary manner. Protective. Possessive.

Peter watched the little tableau, anger rising in his gut. How could she smile at that cretin like he was the last man on earth? He dared Chelios to put his hands on her just once. Jeremy wouldn't have lunch. He wouldn't be able to eat it after Peter finished with him....

"Enjoy your meal, gentlemen," Mary Ellen said, penetrating Peter's brooding. He had no idea what she had talked about. She rose and laid her hand on Chelios's arm. "Thank you, Jeremy."

As she rejoined her own guests, Peter felt the heat rise straight up his neck into his brain. Like steam in a pressure cooker, it found no outlet. He thought he would explode from it.

He was jealous.

Peter blinked, the anger deflating faster than a popped balloon. He couldn't be. Jealousy implied possession and passion. Emotion. He hardly knew Mary Ellen, so how could he be having any feelings toward her? Certainly he knew nothing about her. Okay, he was lustful. It had been a while since his last relationship...about a year. Maybe more.

"Naahh..." he said, astonished.

"You say something, Holiday?"

"No." He cleared his throat. "I was just surprised to hear your daughter had a business lunch. What's her profession?"

"She books women's sports events into the Philadelphia area," Jeremy supplied. "She's very good at finding funding and sponsors, and has an excellent reputation."

"God knows she hits me up enough," Magnussen grumbled, but he bestowed a rare smile on Jeremy.

Peter ground his teeth in frustration. Chelios had done his homework about the family, something Peter hadn't considered. He wouldn't put it past Jeremy to romance Mary Ellen, despite his being married. The man would stop at nothing to fund his study of the eating habits of the Amazonian poison-dart tree frog. The cause might be worthy, but it wouldn't help the world on a grand scale, like his own would.

When lunch broke up, Peter excused himself to use the men's room, although the desire was more emotional than physical. He needed a few moments alone, to get himself under control.

He emerged several minutes later, if not refreshed at least rueful. Unfortunately, Mary Ellen stood by the bank of telephones next to the rest rooms.

"I want to apologize for that kiss the other day," she said. "That was unfair of me. I mean, I don't even know if you have a wife or a girlfriend or...what is it?...a life mate."

"I'm not attached," he said, tucking his doughnut pillow under his arm.

"Really?" She smiled. Delight radiated out from her.

Peter decided the smile she had given Jeremy hadn't been nearly so bright. That suited him fine.

She looked terrific in a red dress and black-and-white checked jacket. The dress hugged her curves, and slender curves they were, too. She had pulled her hair back in a twist. His hands ached to free it and feel the strands play through his fingers.

"Well, I better go," she said, finally moving around him.

He took her arm. "No, wait."

Touching her was a mistake. He wanted to touch more of her. He wanted to make a claim that Jeremy Chelios couldn't break.

He kissed her.

Her lips tasted like chocolate silk. Their tongues touched, then mated as he drew her into his embrace. His hands splayed across her back. He marveled at the fragility and the strength of her flesh. They touched from breast to knee. His head spun.

"What the hell is this?"

Peter sprang away from Mary Ellen, positive he'd been shot again. The mist cleared and, to his horror, he found that John Magnussen stood before them. The man's glare could cut iron. Jeremy glared from right behind him.

"It's not what you think," Peter said hastily. "We were just talking."

"Talk like that produced Mary Ellen."

"Dad, get a grip," Mary Ellen said, her voice dripping with irony. "I'm twenty-eight, a big girl, and it was just a kiss. You can hardly sound like an outraged father in this case, although it's sweet of you to do so.''

Magnussen frowned. "I suppose not."

"You suppose right. I better get back to my guests. They'll be wondering about me. Peter, it was nice kissing you again."

With that bombshell, she walked into the restaurant proper.

Magnussen's gaze swung back to Peter, piercing him with silent accusations. But his only comment was, "I gotta go to the can."

That said more about the situation than anything else, Peter thought. His career was in the toilet now.

Magnussen suited action to words, but Jeremy stayed behind. "Working the daughter is pathetic, Holiday. It will blow up in your face."

"I'm not 'working the daughter,' Chelios," Peter said, curling his hands into fists. "I don't have to. My work stands on its own merits."

"Too bad it doesn't have any."

"The habits of the poisonous tree frog hardly contribute to the saving of humanity, and you know it."

"Neither will your controlling emotional behavior," Jeremy countered. "By the way, I've known the Magnussen family for years, ever since I got my *first* grant from the foundation."

"Don't think that will carry you on this one," Peter said, although he was disconcerted to hear Jeremy had several head starts on the current grant.

"Stay away from Mary Ellen," Jeremy said.

Peter hooted. "What? You gonna tell your wife if I don't?"

"Leave my wife out of this!"

"*You* certainly are." Peter leaned closer and shoved

a finger at Jeremy. "You can lapdog Magnussen all you want, but stay away from Mary Ellen or you'll be spitting Chiclets, pal."

He walked away from Jeremy. He'd heard the words in a movie once, and they sounded right. Certainly the aftermath felt right. Peter's heart pounded. Blood surged through his veins. His brain urged him to follow through on the threat. He wouldn't, of course. He was far too reasonable for violent behavior.

But it felt good. Damn good.

"HI, DAD," Mary Ellen said, kissing her father hello. He had called her to his office, the invitation surprising her. Usually she had to issue them, and usually they were for dinner at her house—when she could pry him out of this place. "What's up?"

"You. Sit down."

She plopped in a chair. "Thanks. I feel like I've been running all day. I've had the women's tennis finals to arrange."

Her father stared at her, not answering. That was a bad sign. He usually tried to intimidate with a look first before speaking. He had the bulk of a wrestler, the stone-faced expression of Ed Sullivan and an overly high forehead due to his balding pate, which only added to his ferocious look. "Ever since you were a little kid, you've tried to get my attention by behavior I couldn't miss if I wanted to. Is that what you're doing now with Peter Holiday?"

Mary Ellen bolted upright. "Dad!"

"Don't 'Dad' me. I know you like to have fun. I know you make it a life's goal, but a simple phone call will achieve the same results. Better, even—"

"All right," she said. "I've heard this one before,

okay? When I was little, yes, I wanted you to pay attention to me and so I was a bad girl who did outrageous things until you looked around and said 'stop.' But I'm a grown-up now. I don't know what the heck you're talking about, but I am *not* doing anything with Peter Holiday to get your attention.''

"Then why were you kissing him the other day at the restaurant?"

"Oh. That." She felt the heat creep into her face. How could she explain what she didn't understand herself? "Dad, I didn't kiss him to get your attention. Or his. Or anyone's. I just…I just wanted to kiss him. He is an attractive man. I can't explain it."

"He's a man who's got a connection to me through the foundation. I can't have that questioned, okay? Especially with the symposium coming up on March first."

"What about Jeremy?" she asked, bristling. "He's been a friend of yours for years. Isn't that a double standard?"

"No. Chelios has attached himself to me, I'll admit that. But I don't encourage it. If you noticed anything, you'll have noticed that he hasn't been around for years, outside of the occasional formal social situation that involves a current grant."

"True," she said, thinking back over how the man had shown up almost continuously during an earlier grant consideration. "He's a suck-up."

"I know what he is. But that doesn't change his science project, which is pretty good. So is Holiday's on emotional behavior. I don't want you ruining this for anybody."

"I'm not getting involved with him, believe me."

She waved a hand. "He and I have different philosophies of life."

She wanted to urge her father to drop Peter from the grant consideration because of that philosophy. The man wanted to eliminate love. Maybe she felt so strongly because she'd shot him with an arrow on Valentine's Day. Maybe Cupid had invaded her psyche or something, but she, who never cared about the grant foundation—who never understood half the projects it funded—didn't want love touched. Yet she kept silent. Surely her father could see the dangers she saw. And it wouldn't be fair for her to exert any influence she might have with him. Knowing her dad, he would probably give the grant to Peter just because she protested. He still thought of her as a little kid. Hence today's summons.

"I just wanted to be sure," her father conceded. "A guy like Peter doesn't understand undercurrents. These scientists are innocents in social situations, believe me. You fool around with him, Mary Ellen, and you'll break his heart."

"I have no interest," she said self-righteously. She meant it too. Well, maybe a physical interest, a chemical one. But she certainly wouldn't act on it. Not even an unorthodox Valentine's Day meeting would change that.

"Well, take care of it, okay? I don't want any problems between Holiday and you."

"I promise." She meant it.

MARY ELLEN PUSHED through the doors of the low building, surprised by the Quonset hut feel of the Eastern Pennsylvania Behavioral Center.

Inside, the center looked spacious and modern—except for its high curved ceiling, which reminded her of a wine cellar in an Italian castle.

A young man in the requisite lab coat and glasses bustled up to her. "No unauthorized admittance!"

Mary Ellen smiled sweetly. "I'm here to see Dr. Holiday."

"Why?"

"Personal business."

"What personal business?"

Mary Ellen was tempted to say it wouldn't be personal if she told him, but the point would probably be lost. Instead, she said, "I'm a strip-o-gram here for his birthday. He's getting the *full* treatment."

His mouth formed a perfect O of astonishment.

"Mary Ellen?"

Peter stood in an office doorway. His expression nearly matched the young man's.

Mary Ellen smiled. "Hi, Peter. How's the behind?"

"You'll never let me forget that, will you?"

"*I'll* never forget it, that's for sure."

"She *says* she's a stripper for your birthday," the young man said in a suspicious tone.

"My birthday's not until August, Matthew."

Matthew flushed. "Oh. Right."

"I believe it's time to feed Roxanne."

Matthew disappeared behind some partitions.

"Sorry about that," Mary Ellen said. "He was rude and I couldn't resist."

"You probably made his decade. But don't mind Matthew. He's always been abrupt, though he's thorough in his work. In fact, he handles most of the daily work for me as my assistant. I don't know if I could have gotten this far without him."

Peter gazed at her with that same look he had at the

restaurant. Mary Ellen resisted the urge to melt against him. One time had created enough trouble already.

"I, ah, I came to apologize for the, um, compromising position at the restaurant."

She was always apologizing to this man. If love meant never having to say you're sorry, then she was definitely in lust, thank goodness. Still, her father's lecture about the perils of toying with innocent scientists rattled in her brain. She had thought about his admonitions for a few days and decided she ought to straighten out the situation once and for all.

"I believe I was responsible for the restaurant incident," Peter said.

"Probably we both were. I just wanted you to know it won't affect your chances for the grant."

He sucked in his breath. "What the hell did you do?"

"Nothing! Well, I talked to my father—"

"God, no! That was the worst thing you could have done!"

"Relax." She grinned ruefully. "He blames me entirely. I got a lecture about being impulsive with naive men."

"I'm hardly naive."

Mary Ellen snorted. "My father thinks you're positively virginal. That's not a bad thing in this case, Peter."

"Maybe." He hardly looked appeased. She supposed no man felt that way when his sexuality came into question. She had refrained from telling her father that Peter's seemed fine to her. No sense rocking the boat more. Besides, she was unprepared to deal with sexuality and Peter Holiday.

"I've wanted to apologize to you," he said. "I did create that compromising position, after all. My fault."

"What an apology-fest we have going here." She brightened. "Show me around, will you? I'd love to see what you do."

"Are you sure?"

"Sure."

"I'm not sure. We seem to be on a collision course whenever we meet."

"One arrow and you think the world is falling apart."

"It is." But he smiled. "Come on. Maybe you won't be so skeptical when you see what I'm doing."

"That's my hope," she muttered dubiously, following him into the center's working areas. Maybe if she knew more about his project, she wouldn't have this knee-jerk reaction. Maybe. It was worth a try.

She noticed he walked with a slight limp, a remnant of their first encounter. Guilt whacked at her again. Cupid couldn't have found a better mark, only her strike hadn't been for love. She would find the best of what his job entailed, to make up for this.

To her surprise, she saw computers rather than cages, other than a spacious one with some cute white mice running around happily in it. Peter explained that the creatures were helping him with what he thought was a breakthrough. Mary Ellen looked at the mice curiously. They seemed normal.

People in jeans and sweatshirts sat before the green glare of computer monitors. Others sat in cubicles or offices, heads bent over papers and printouts. Peter showed Mary Ellen several compilations of various interviews with test subjects. The tests themselves focused on such mundane issues as the spending and eat-

ing habits of humans over a long span of time. Roxanne
turned out to be a cat, the free-roaming pet of the fa-
cility and not some downtrodden chimp used for ne-
farious experiments.

They ran into Matthew, who was engrossed in a conversation with a woman. He actually smiled.

"This is so normal," Mary Ellen said, when they
reached Peter's office.

Peter chuckled. "What were you expecting? Bill
Murray zapping students to impress a girl?"

She gaped in awe. "You've seen *Ghostbusters*!"

"I'm not a total geek," Peter said. "I like movies.
Don't tell anyone, but I like the *Police Academy*
series."

"Here I thought you wouldn't know what a movie
is, let alone *Police Academy*."

"They went downhill after Guttenberg was gone."

"You really do know the movies! Okay, who starred
in *Airheads*?"

"Brendan Fraser. He was great in *Encino Man*. Of
course, the science was all wrong—"

"Who cares? It was great fun. Do you know *Class
Act*?"

"Kid 'n' Play. *House Party* was better. So was Kid's
hair then."

She sucked in her breath. "You enjoy all the movies
that the critics say we're not suppose to. Just like me."

He smiled. "We have something in common."

She walked around the small room, fascinated with
the clutter. She would have expected neat piles of papers and pens set at precise angles to desk pads. Instead, it reminded her of her own office, only without
the basketballs and tennis rackets stacked on filing cab-
inets. *Just like her*. The behavioral scientist had normal

quirks, making him very human. And more attractive than before. The ring sat on his chair, obviously ready for duty. She smiled at it.

A wall photo caught her eye. "My God! You knew Einstein!"

He laughed. "That's Walter Matthau on the set of *IQ*. Einstein died in 1955. How could I be a grown man in the picture if I wasn't even born yet? Think about it."

"Oh, the heck with chronology. You were on the set of *IQ*? That must have been neat."

"One of my finest moments." He came over to her. "They filmed part of it at Princeton. I knew someone who got me a meeting with the cast. Walter was really nice. All of them were."

"Did you meet Meg Ryan, too?"

"Yes. She's much taller than I expected."

"It's the camera. It makes you look bigger than you are."

"So I found out. I was an extra in the ice-cream scene. My mother called me afterward and told me I needed to lose weight."

"Wow. I'm with a movie star. I'm impressed, Dr. Holiday." She was impressed—and very surprised.

"I'm glad I've impressed you with something."

She turned to him. "Believe me, you have."

His gaze grew darker, more piercing.

"This got us into trouble before," she said, alarms going off in her head. Her body had other ideas.

"You're right." Only he didn't move.

"Oh, hell," she muttered, pulling him to her.

This kiss held fire from the moment their lips touched. Their tongues mated fiercely. She pressed herself to him, not surprised to feel his ready response.

His hands swept down her back. Strong hands. Gentle hands. His fingers sunk into her derriere, kneading her flesh. God, but it felt so good. He felt so good. She curled her hands into his shoulders, feeling the strength in them. So surprising for a scientist, she thought. Unexpected. She liked these hidden facets of him. Her blood thickened and pulsed. Her heart beat faster. She pressed impossibly closer. If this was a chemical imbalance, then she didn't want the cure.

That thought reminded her of a basic disagreement between them. He didn't believe in love, only mating urges that held no lifetime commitment. She, on the other hand, had suffered love's ups and downs, and come through it a better person. Love was life. And to take away love was to take away life.

Mary Ellen pulled out of his embrace. "I think I owe you another apology. I shouldn't have done that."

"I owe you one, too. I can't deny I was a willing participant."

"Me, too."

"Very willing."

"Me, too."

That he had been willing pushed her over some edge she'd barely been hanging on to. She threw herself at him this time, their mouths almost mashing together in their eagerness to kiss. She forgot their differing philosophies. Besides, how could philosophy survive the onslaught of gonads?

He lifted her off her feet, his hands under her behind. He stumbled over to a counter and laid her down on the cool marble top. He buried his face in her breasts, the counter's height clearly allowing him access without bending and aggravating his wound.

"This is all wrong," she whispered, guiding his

head from one breast to the other. Clothes were no barrier to the sensations running rampant inside her.

"Anyone could come in here," he muttered, pulling her sweater out of her trousers and pushing it up to her chest.

"Anyone?"

"Anyone."

"Then let's be quick."

He pushed up her soft bra. Cool air turned her nipples to diamond points. She yanked his shirt open in turn. Hair covered his chest and arrowed down past his waist.

"Oh, God," she moaned, running her fingers through the silken patch.

His mouth turned her to fire. His skin burned her hands. He burned for her. She could feel it.

Somewhere an unwanted caution managed to fight through the out-of-control urges. She tried to ignore it. She couldn't.

"Peter," she gasped, breathless from his ministrations, yet trying to get his attention.

"Yes. Say my name."

"Oh." She started laughing. "No, Peter, not that. Well, yes, that." She pushed at him. "We have to stop."

He paused. "We do?"

"Yes. Think about it."

"Damn." He rested his head on her chest for a long moment, then straightened, letting her go.

Mary Ellen pushed her clothes down over her bare skin, saying, "Here comes another apology."

"Stop!" He looked stricken. "Every time you apologize, we wind up like people too long on a desert island."

"You're right." She sat up and pushed her fingers through her hair, trying to settle it into some order. "I don't understand this."

"Neither do I. I have never acted like this with a woman before."

"That sounds suspiciously like an apology."

"Sorry."

"Yikes." She grew serious. "This is not my normal behavior either, I assure you. Maybe it's Cupid. We did meet on Valentine's Day, after all."

"Don't be ridiculous. Valentine was a martyred bishop, although his being a symbol of love actually enhances my point about it definitely being a chemical imbalance—"

"Don't start." She slid off the desk.

"I do want you to know my actions are not designed to seduce you in order to get to your father."

She glanced up in surprise. "I never thought that. Why would I? I sought you out today."

"True." He smiled.

"Why would you ever think I would think that?" she asked curiously.

"I just want to be clear."

"I guess people could get the wrong impression." *What an understatement,* she thought.

Awkward silence ensued. She finally said, "I'd better go."

He escorted her to the front door.

"I enjoyed the tour," she said, to be polite, then made a wry face. "That's stepping in it."

"We've done that enough as it is."

"Goodbye, Peter." She meant it. She wouldn't see him again.

"Goodbye." He looked as resolute as she tried to feel.

She wanted to kiss him, but knew that would be foolish. Instead, she waved, a lame gesture compared to the heat they'd generated in his office.

Later, in her own office, she decided she should give him a peace offering. Not an apology, she hastily assured herself; that was dangerous. She wasn't weakening from her earlier resolve not to see him, either. She just wanted a simple—what?—sign of friendship between them?

Mary Ellen grinned. She liked that.

She called in her assistant. "Sally. I want you to send one of the comp tickets for the women's college basketball tournament to Dr. Peter Holiday." The tournament was Mary Ellen's pet project, and she was damn proud of it. She gave Sally the address. "I'm sorry. I don't have the zip. You'll have to look that up."

"No problem."

A simple apology without complications, she thought. Why couldn't she and Peter do that?

Sally turned to leave.

"Send him two," Mary Ellen said, making a quick decision.

Sally noted it and left the room.

Maybe Peter would want to bring a friend, Mary Ellen thought. Maybe a woman friend. The idea sent a shaft of pain into her heart.

Maybe he would bring Matthew.

That would be nice. Very nice.

Chapter Three

Peter made his way into the crowded stands, surprised to find the Corestate Center packed for a woman's basketball game.

His seat was three rows from the floor. He had an excellent view. Only one question disturbed him: why was he here?

"Huskies! Woof, woof, woof!" his neighbor barked, startling him. More barking erupted around Peter, even though the game hadn't yet begun.

Peter glanced at the young man, who wore a University of Connecticut T-shirt, his face painted half blue, half white. Peter wondered whether he was at a basketball game or a Polynesian tribal ritual. He set his doughnut pillow on the seat, then sat on it. Ever since that explosion of passion in his office, his posterior ached. He hoped he hadn't redamaged the wound. He had no desire for that form of poetic justice.

Unfortunately, the rest of him ached for Mary Ellen. He hoped they hadn't opened a floodgate of passion better left closed, but he was afraid they had. Cupid better not have shot that arrow. Peter reprimanded himself for foolish thinking. Cupid didn't enter into it.

So why was Peter here, using her tickets? He'd

asked himself the question with every step he had taken—and come up with no answer other than stupidity. Probably he wouldn't see her at all tonight. He *was* curious about her job. He had time on his hands, too. The symposium had been postponed because of a blizzard on March first. Now he had more time to work. The postponement played to his cause especially well.   Magnussen hadn't set a new date just yet. Two weeks extra would be good. A month would be even better.

"You planning to stay for the entire tournament?" his neighbor asked. "That's a pretty good way to keep from getting a sore butt."

"I had an accident," Peter explained. "May I ask why you've painted your face like that?"

"School colors, man! Show your pride. U-Conn Huskies! Woof! Woof! Woof!"

"Yes, I understand that," Peter said. "But isn't that dangerous to the skin?"

"Nah. It's water-based paint."

"I see."

"Carolina, Carolina, Carolina!"

The chant from the other side of the arena erupted. The young man leapt up and began "woofing" at the top of his lungs, exhorting the surrounding rows to do the same.

When his seatmate sat down, Peter asked him about a curiosity he'd noticed on the tickets. "Why is the University of Connecticut playing Carolina State in Philadelphia?"

"March Madness," the student answered cryptically. He added, "The playoffs of the basketball season are always held on a neutral site. Keeps teams from having home-court advantage."

"Good point," Peter said.

Fascinated, he watched the rival college crowds work themselves up into a frenzy of classic mob behavior as the game begun. He noticed many more painted faces, both male and female, among the spectators. Maybe he couldn't explain the compulsion to use Mary Ellen's tickets, but he had to thank her for them. She'd opened a whole new world of study—sports spectators. To think he hadn't planned to come at all, but had had a last-minute change of heart.

Peter made a bet with himself on how long it would take before the frenzy turned to violence. To his further surprise, only a few fights broke out. The security guards quickly removed the individuals.

He found himself watching the players, too. The women's faces held a determination that must have mirrored those of the Spartans at Thermopylae, when that small, valiant group held off thousands of Persians from invading ancient Greece. The women's bodies were strong, yet lithe. Of course, next to Mary Ellen's, these did nothing for him.

Wonderful, Peter thought, disgusted that he even made the comparison. He *had* to get a grip on himself.

"You came!"

Mary Ellen stood at the bottom of the seating tiers, on the edge of the court. She wore a sedate gray suit, a large plastic badge clipped to the lapel. Several people yelled at her for blocking their view. She raised a forefinger, signaling for him to wait, then scurried around to the stairs. She squeezed in front of the people in his row until she reached the empty seat next to him.

"I'll visit for a few moments until your guest comes back," she said, sitting down.

Her perfume teased his senses. "I didn't bring a guest."

She grinned. "Then I'll visit longer. I heard the symposium got canceled because of the snowstorm."

"Yes. I don't know when it's being rescheduled for. Have you heard?"

She shrugged. "My father's in Scotland for a couple of weeks on business. He'll probably set it up when he comes back. Are you enjoying the tourney?"

"It's fascinating." His neighbor nudged him. Peter said, "Excuse me," and stood up with everyone else around them. He shouted in chorus with the others, "Huskies! Woof, woof, woof!"

"My, you are fascinated," Mary Ellen said, laughing. "What behavior from the behavioral scientist."

That he was here proved that. He didn't believe in love or a lifetime commitment to the emotion, yet this woman intrigued him. He liked to hear her laugh. He liked to look at her face.

"Follow the mob, I always say," he said. "Besides, my alma mater isn't known for its sports programs."

"Where was that?"

"Harvard."

"It figures."

"We do have a good ice hockey team," he said defensively. "I think."

She laughed again. "You'll be dangerous when you actually get on the planet."

"So I've been told." He glanced around. "I have to say that this is an amazing turnout for women's basketball, especially in a place that's not connected to either team. I had no idea it was popular."

"It's the up-and-coming sport of the nineties. CBS has picked it up for its Saturday broadcasts. Ratings for women's ball is excellent. ESPN has been showing it for years now. The gate is great, too."

"The gate?"

"Attendance," she explained. "And that means ticket sales, and that's money. Women's tennis became mainstream in the seventies, followed by women's golf. Besides the women's pro and college basketball tourneys, I now have deals for women's indoor track-and-field, fast-pitch softball and volleyball to come to Philadelphia."

"Fascinating." That seemed to be his catchword tonight, but he *was* fascinated. "And you believe those sports will bring in the general population as well? Excuse me." Peter stood and "woofed" again with the crowd.

She doubled over with laughter. "Oh, Peter. I have to send you more tickets."

"Thank you. I would like to study the behavior patterns of sports spectators. Further close-hand views would be instructive."

"You're in your professor mode. I can tell."

"Doctor."

"Whatever. Are your brothers and sisters like you?"

"I'm an only child, although I have some cousins I'm close to. Michael, Jared and Raymond are all close to me in age. My father has three brothers—their fathers—and a sister, but there aren't many Holidays of my generation. Just the four of us, my cousins and I."

"An only child—each one of you. That explains a lot."

He frowned. "I'm not repressed. Neither are my cousins. Do you have any siblings?"

"An older sister who lives in California."

"Oh."

She hooted with mirth again. He was still the comic relief, and there wasn't an arrow in sight.

"You *know* I'm not repressed."

She sobered. That was better.

He asked the question that had puzzled him for some time now. "Why did you send me the tickets? I was surprised to receive them."

A woman in a blue jacket with a school patch on the pocket motioned to Mary Ellen from the aisle. "Kyle called. He said to call back pronto," the woman yelled, loudly enough to be heard over the crowd. "It's an emergency."

"Hell's bells," Mary Ellen muttered, waving in acknowledgment to the woman. "I have to go."

"Okay." Disappointment crept through Peter. He shouldn't feel that, he thought. And who the hell was Kyle?

"Why don't you come with me, and I'll show you my office after I'm finished with Kyle? I owe you a tour."

"Look what happened at the last one."

"Chicken."

"Not me. Woof, woof, woof. Okay."

Following her lead, he tucked his pillow under his arm and made his way down the row, apologizing out loud, but silently wondering if he were living dangerously. He could control his emotions. He was a grown man and had no excuse not to.

Mary Ellen led him down into the bowels of the building. People bustled through a rabbit warren of offices. She entered one. Its door held the same symbol as the patch on the other woman's jacket. Peter realized the school logo was actually Mary Ellen's company logo. To his relief and consternation, her office was as cluttered as his. While he didn't lose self-esteem for his slapdash habits, he wished she were a neat freak. Anything to turn him off.

"My office is another sign of women's sports becoming more significant," she said. "They've given it a separate branch from the promotions department. Of course, I had to campaign like hell for it."

She waved him into a chair while she picked up the telephone. He gathered from the conversation that "Kyle" had encountered a hitch in lining up tennis stars for a match next year. Mary Ellen was calm but adamant. Her sternness surprised Peter. He had thought her ditzy. Now he saw another side to her. How many more were there?

She, too, papered her walls with pictures. Many were of her standing with people he assumed were sports figures. They wore team uniforms, so he thought his guess a decent one. Several photos were of her and her father. One was of her and Jeremy. They were arm in arm.

Peter's blood pressure shot up and his head began to throb.

"Sometimes tennis people are the worst," she said, hanging up the telephone.

He grunted, still staring at the offensive picture. "I didn't know you had a relationship with Jeremy Chelios."

"Who?" She came over to the picture. "Oh. Actually, Jeremy's a friend of my father's. Sort of. Acquaintance is more like it, according to Dad. Jeremy was here with him at the ground-breaking ceremony, several years back. That's the only photo I have of this building then."

A likely story, Peter thought, but didn't voice it. His

rival for the grant looked as though he had inside connections on behalf of his tree frogs.

"I'll show you around."

Peter walked behind her, fighting the twin urges to feel the soft flesh of her derriere and do something more violent. Either reaction was completely unlike him. The only explanation that made sense *was* a chemical imbalance of the brain. How could it be anything else? The irony that he was his own best example of the phenomenon was not lost on him. Good thing he'd found what looked like an antidote for the imbalance. Right now, the mice were testing it. If these uncontrollable urges about Mary Ellen didn't stop, he'd be taking the stuff himself, and to hell with the control studies.

She showed him weight-lifting rooms, equipment rooms and locker rooms galore. The first-aid station was a miracle of modern medicine, with equipment other struggling scientists he knew would kill to have. In fact, the multimillion-dollar facilities put his own converted Quonset hut to shame.

"Very impressive," he said when they returned to her office. He meant it.

"You sound disappointed."

"Envious," he admitted freely. That stupid picture taunted him from the wall, seeming to grow larger and larger until he could see the lust in Chelios's eyes. They mocked Peter with their possessiveness. "You and Jeremy must be very close."

"What?"

He pointed to the picture. "He's married, you know."

"His wife is lovely, and no, while I know Jeremy, we're hardly close. Acquaintances at best."

"Then why have his picture on the wall?"

"I told you, that's the only one I have of the ground-breaking ceremony."

"Surely the center here has ground-breaking-ceremony photos. You ought to easily get one of them. If that's all the picture means to you."

"What's with you?" she demanded, glaring at him.

"I'm just pointing out illogical behavior," he said, determined to mean it. "I only have pictures on my walls that are of people important to me. That's the logical reason to hang a photo in one's office."

"Pay attention." She pointed to five pictures in a row, the one with Jeremy being the first. "This shows the ground breaking. This the steel skeleton. The next the outer walls going up, then the roof and finally opening day. If you'll notice, I'm in every picture with my arm around someone. I wanted to be in them, for my own satisfaction, and I wanted to show size perspective. I'm with three women in the far-right photo. Did you think I was having an orgy?"

"Don't be ridiculous!" he said, staring at the pictorial chronicle of the Corestate Center building process.

"You're jealous!"

He gaped at her. She couldn't be right. She was right. "Don't be ridiculous!"

He said the words too late. He knew it and she knew it. He could have handed over ammo to a mad general and achieved the same results.

She grinned and strolled toward him. "You can deny it, but you know you are. Jealousy is sweet."

"Obviously, it's a chemical imbalance," he began, horrified that she found his nonsensical reaction "sweet."

"Then let's unbalance you more."

She took him by his lapels and pulled him against her. She kissed him.

SHE MEANT TO TEASE HIM a little, to give in to the exhilaration of knowing he felt some possessiveness toward her and to show him how nonsensical he was being about emotions.

The moment her lips touched his, however, her own emotions spun out of control. His "chemical imbalances," his clear lack of commitment to a relationship, even her father's warnings didn't matter. She only wanted to touch and taste him. He didn't even put up a semblance of denial in the kiss. His tongue found hers immediately. Mary Ellen melted against him. His arms wrapped around her, holding her up.

They strung endless kisses together, no sooner breaking one than beginning all over again. Her blood was on fire, like molten lava pulsing in her veins. Her breasts ached for his touch. She throbbed deep inside.

He turned her and swept her desk clear, the clatter of pens, papers and lamp falling to the floor like music to her ears. He laid her on the desktop, wincing slightly with the pain. She kissed him, little tiny kisses of apology. She had a tournament going on upstairs and a million things that required her attention. Yet Peter was here, and only that mattered now.

"Will we be interrupted?" he asked.

She reached up and began to unbutton his shirt. "Nope."

"Good."

He got her blouse open, with a little fumbling. She loved the lack of finesse. It said much about his honest emotions, even if he didn't recognize them. His hands caressed her breasts, followed by his mouth. Mary Ellen moaned. He was so different from other men she encountered. Maybe a little too different. She didn't care. He felt so good…

Someone pounded on her door.

Peter yelped and scrambled off her. She scrambled up after him, bumping him off balance.

"Who is it?" she called out, while grabbing Peter to steady him.

"Joanne. Are you all right in there?"

"Fine, fine." Mary Ellen tried to button her blouse with shaky fingers.

Joanne opened the door. She took one look at the clutter on the floor, the cleared desk, Peter's still-open shirt and Mary Ellen's half-buttoned one. A flush crept up the woman's cheeks, while she grinned a silly smile. She only said, "We're having a problem with the food service again."

"Okay." Mary Ellen died a thousand deaths even as she gave a nonchalant answer. Joanne would spread the news all over the center before five minutes were up. If she were Joanne, she would.

Joanne left and Peter said, "We wouldn't be interrupted?"

"I'm never in my office during my events. Everyone knows that." Mary Ellen finally managed to fasten the last few buttons. "At least everyone used to know it. I'm sorry."

"Don't say that!"

"Stop being superstitious," she said. "Love means never having to say you're sorry. Remember that movie?"

"Couldn't go by us." He ran his fingers through his

hair. "The tickets were an apology, too, weren't they? That would explain a lot."

"They were a peace offering."

"A technicality."

"I have to go." What the hell was she doing? She never attacked men like this. She didn't understand herself at all. "Look, Mr. Bright Guy, we clearly have a problem of attraction. Yet you and I don't even believe in the same things about it. I think we ought to kill this chemical imbalance with a date."

"A date?"

"You don't have to make it sound as if I want you to wear a full-length mink to an animal-activists convention. It would be a simple dinner to discuss this, okay?"

He hesitated. "Okay, but a dinner only. No date and no apology."

"Deal."

She left him in the office while she escaped to solve the food-service problem. When she returned, he was gone. She knew it was just as well. She had nearly talked herself into an apology in the interim.

THE NEXT NIGHT, they drove separately to dinner and even agreed to split the bill. No date. Intense discussion began with dessert.

"I truly can't explain my behavior toward you," he said. "I lose control of myself somehow. This is not an excuse. I just don't excuse it. I don't understand it."

"I don't understand it, either," she admitted. Truly she didn't. Whenever he was near her, something happened. Of all the men to be attracted to, she had to go and get attracted to one who believed long-term commitment was a mistake of nature. "Maybe it really is

Cupid at work or something. After all, I shot you in the butt on Valentine's Day. That's got to be significant.''

"I wish I could blame such a thing as a Cupid. But the only significance to your arrow shot is that you have bad aim."

"But I don't. That's the point."

"I got the point." He tapped the doughnut ring under his butt. "It wasn't from good aim."

She waved a hand. "How we met doesn't matter anymore. All I know is that it started something. Obviously, we're attracted to each other. You call it a chemical imbalance. I call it force of nature. Chemical imbalance or not, what are we going to do about it?"

"You can stop sending peace offerings for one thing," he said. "If I want to study the behavior of sports spectators, I'll do it without free tickets from you."

"All right. We could stop apologizing, too, just on the off chance you are right and it triggers something. If I shoot you in the butt again, I'll just say, 'Oh, well,' and go on to the next shot."

"God knows where that will land."

"In the bull's-eye, I hope." She gazed at him, her coffee cup halfway to her mouth. A crazy idea occurred to her. "Maybe we ought to give in to this to see where it leads. Maybe it will get it all out of our systems, rather than making it seem forbidden."

"No." He shook his head. "Your father's giving a grant I've applied for. It would be improper and unethical for us to further any personal relationship until the decision is made."

"I love it when you go all professional. You're probably right, however." She never had liked proper behavior. Her mother had always emphasized ladylike manners and sitting quietly. Mary Ellen eventually realized both were used as tools for her mother to ignore her children. Proper behavior always seemed more like Chinese water torture after that. But Mary Ellen wouldn't jeopardize Peter's chances with any improper behavior, even if she disagreed with his theories about love. That wouldn't be fair, and she did try to always play fair. "Okay, so we're agreed that this is completely wrong for us personally and also professionally."

"Right."

"No more apologies or peace offerings."

"Exactly."

"We're miles apart philosophically, since you're brains and I'm brawn."

"Somehow my male ego took a hit with that...but yes."

"You think love is an emotion to be eradicated—"

"I think love and other emotions need to be controlled in order to take mankind to the next level of civilization. Let's keep it in perspective."

"Right. You think love should be eradicated. I think, despite love's drawbacks, mankind needs it and all our other emotions to keep us from falling back into a zombie state. Now that's perspective."

He looked heavenward for help.

She continued to lay out their problems. "Behavior is everything, and we must behave like mature adults."

He eyed her. "We are behaving like two mature adults. That's our problem."

"Sorry. I mean, right."

"You do like to live on the edge, don't you?"

She grinned ruefully. "I try. You know it's not the apologies that are doing it."

"Our timing says otherwise."

"You're the behavior expert. You cure us." She brightened. "Hey! If it works, then my father will definitely give you the grant."

"What we're experiencing is lust, not love, although I'd be tempted to take up your suggestion if my prototype antidote was fully tested."

"It was a thought." She gazed at him, a myriad of emotions spinning through her, lust not the foremost. He'd mentioned an antidote before, but the notion of it scared her now. Surely he couldn't really cure love? Yet even thinking he might didn't stop her attraction to him. Even now, just looking at his face, she wanted to trace every line, to memorize each little bump and groove, to discover the way the cragginess came together into handsome features.... She wanted to stare into his blue eyes, piercing like ice in their color. She wanted to run her fingers through his thick hair.

Okay, so he looked good. She didn't know a lot about him, other than their mutual enjoyment of movies. Maybe if she found out more, she wouldn't have this compelling urge to ignore their agreement. Just to be on the safe side, she'd make sure they were incompatible. "Tell me you don't like hot-fudge sundaes."

"I do. With nuts."

"Do you read the Sunday paper from cover to cover?"

"Including the For Sale items."

"Oh, God. Which do you like—cats or dogs?"

He cleared his throat. "Neither, really. I was a fish kid."

"Oh, God, no." She stared at him, stricken. "You like all the things I like. You can't."

"What's your point?"

"We have things in common. Things that could make us compatible."

"Convicted murderers probably like hot-fudge sundaes and have fish for pets. That doesn't mean either of us is compatible with them, believe me."

He had a point. Only she had a feeling that the more she probed, the more she would find she liked about him. She needed a downer, something to tell her this was all wrong. "Tell me why you don't like love."

"I don't like or dislike it. It's simply a controllable imbalance of the brain, and many people suffer its consequences when it goes bad."

"Something must have put you on this path. Something made you look beyond the emotion."

He frowned, clearly thinking about the question. "Well…maybe one thing. When I was a child, my grandmother left my grandfather for another man. She was obsessed with this gentleman, like she had a second youth. He left her eventually, and she was so devastated, she tried to kill herself. Her life and my grandfather's life with her was ruined forever. The whole family's, really, because it affected their children and their grandchildren, of which I was one. I loved her, and I loved my grandfather very much. He was incredibly hurt by her betrayal, and he was never the same man again. I remember being so confused about what had happened. My cousins, too. We used to spend our summers with them at their house near the shore in Wildwood. It was great fun…until my grandmother's affair." He chuckled. "I can laugh about it now, but back then Michael, Jared, Raymond and I were so upset that we took a solemn vow not to love anyone. We were just kids. My father used to say to me afterward that he was smart to not have married for love. I have to admit that as I studied the effects of emotional behavior and whether it was a physiological phenomenon that could be controlled, I gravitated toward trying to find an explanation for my grandmother's obsession. No doubt the family happening started me on my work, but I've gone way beyond it.''

How incredibly hurt he must have been over his grandparents, she thought. He must have really loved them with a child's very special love. To have it all snatched away because of an adult situation that he never would have understood at the time had been bewildering and devastating. Worse, his own parents had a loveless marriage, the father emphasizing that love was bad and giving Peter a living example to follow. Mary Ellen's heart broke for the boy he had been. He was still trying to fix his grandparents' relationship, too. Her heart broke for the man.

"Nobody ever knows what truly happens in a marriage," she said. "Maybe she married your grandfather on the rebound from this guy in the first place. Maybe your grandfather didn't treat her as well privately as he did publicly. People hide a lot of things. I love my father, but he's a workaholic, and my mother eventually left him, after I was on my own. Their only connection was me, and when I was gone, they had nothing together but a lifetime of sniping and complaining. I love them both, and the divorce was devastating, but they had never developed a life together to begin with. Actually, they had the kind of marriage you want to create, because they had all kinds of life-style compat-

ibility. Even with compatibility it can be just as devastating to families as your chemical imbalance.''

"Your parents are a unique case," he said. "Most
people with compatibility have a naturally created life
together because they mutually agree on basic life-
styles. It works better, believe me."

Mary Ellen wondered about their own compatibility.
She could envision quiet nights snuggled with him in
front of the television, with an intellectually "forbidden" movie and a bowl of popcorn. She could easily
see Sunday mornings lying around the living room
trading and reading every oversize section of the newspaper. And hot-fudge sundaes… Her heart swelled with
emotion. That response was dangerous, too. He didn't
have the same emotions as she did.

"I better go," she said.

"Me, too."

They split the check and tip, although he protested.
They walked out to the parking lot together. Their foot-
steps crunched through the snow left over from the
blizzard. Mary Ellen liked snow. Stars shone brightly
in the cold night air. She liked the night sky, too, but
its brilliance depressed her now. Why should she feel
depressed when common sense prevailed?

She pointed to the right. "My car's over there."

He gestured in the opposite direction. "Mine's this
way."

She faced him. "I guess this is goodbye."

"Yes."

"I really have this urge to kiss you." She wanted to
be honest with him. For all their disagreement about
life and love, they had been honest with each other.
Brutally so.

"Me, too."

She chuckled. "You want to kiss you?"

"No. I want to kiss *you*."

Hearing him say it made her put action to words. She stretched up. Just their lips touched. Their other kisses had been spurred from moments of passion, but this one held a poignancy that broke her heart. But her heart hadn't been involved in this, so how could it feel broken?

Her head spun when they eased their mouths away. "I—I...better go."

"Me, too."

They stood for another moment, awkward with each other. Finally he moved, and she found herself released from some crazy spell. She walked away from him without looking back. She got in her car and drove home. With each passing minute, however, a compulsion grew within her to discover where he really stood on their agreement. Not what his mouth said, but what his heart said. She had to know that, like her, his heart ached, too. She couldn't explain the notion—and it shouldn't matter at all, because they disagreed about love—but she couldn't shake it.

She tried to control the urge, to push it aside. It ate at her. She made a few phone calls, just for the heck of it, and discovered his home address easily. He lived in the next Philadelphia suburb. That pushed her over the edge. Common sense be damned.

She found his house without too much difficulty. Midnight wasn't the best time for this, but she had to know. He answered her second knock. He gaped at her. She wanted to gape at him, for he wore only a bathrobe. Between the bare chest showing above the crisscrossing panels of terry cloth and the bare calves and feet, he sure looked naked to her.

"Mary Ellen! What are you doing here?"

"A good question." She seized the bull by the horns. "Look, do you really like this agreement we've made?"

"Well...I agreed to it."

His hesitation buoyed her. "Yes. So did I. Common sense, propriety, difference of opinions and all that. But do you personally like it?"

He didn't say anything for the longest time. "I hate it."

"Thank God. I hate it, too."

She stepped inside, pulled him to her and kissed him. He shut the door behind them.

Chapter Four

"Oh, Mary Ellen," Peter muttered, running his hands down her back and spreading kisses on her neck.

The moment they had parted at the restaurant, he had hungered for her like a sailor too long alone at sea. Now she pressed against him, alive and real. No dream. No illusion. He hoped.

"I went crazy after I left the restaurant. I was ready to beat down your office door first thing in the morning." He admitted a further truth. "I didn't think I would survive the night."

She chuckled. "Instead, I beat down your door."

"How did you find me?" Even as he spoke, his hands were busy stripping off her jacket.

"I have friends at the phone company." Her fingers pushed open the upper folds of his robe. She placed one palm against his chest.

Peter sucked in his breath. Her touch sent his senses spinning. "This is insane."

"I know."

Her agreement didn't help his common sense. He yanked her sweater over her head. Her skin felt like pure silk to his palms. Her lacy bra veiled her dark areolas, hinting at them in the most seductive of ways. He crushed her in his arms and kissed her fiercely.

Their tongues dueled in the promise of the mating of bodies. Their mouths twisted and turned, sucking and caressing. When their lips finally eased away, they stared at each other in shock—then kissed again and again.

Peter lifted her in his arms, feeling strong, stronger than the strongest man in the world. The stairs loomed, the bed beyond them. Doubt crept into his mind. Mary Ellen curled her tongue across the arch of his throat. That did it.

He practically ran up the stairs and into his bedroom. He fell with her onto the bed. They came up laughing and gasping for air.

"Wow! Big, strong man carry woman upstairs," Mary Ellen quipped.

Peter nuzzled her cheek. "Now big, strong man have hernia."

"No kidding. I can't wait to hear you explain this behavior."

"You bring out the animal in me?"

She started laughing. "Oh, Lord. I can't wait to find out which one."

"Rabbit."

They laughed together, then sobered. Somewhere in Peter's head, a voice reminded him of morality and grants and conscience. He quite sensibly told the voice to go to hell, and kissed Mary Ellen breathless. He could say all he wanted about human emotional behavior, but nothing explained the compulsion, the deep need, the desperate wanting to be with Mary Ellen. He could only follow each to its completion.

He got her clothes off with a minimum of fumbling—a victory for him, considering he felt like a boy with his first woman. But her mouth was cool fire and her hands urged him on. He had only to look at her half-closed eyes to know she wanted him as much as he wanted her. She was beautiful, as beautiful as Botticelli's *Venus,* yet her sprinkling of freckles making her the girl next door.

He ran his hands up and down every inch of her naked flesh. His exploration delighted him and left him awestruck at the female form. Her form. She had curves and softness, a feminine strength that teased and challenged him. He could never have guessed a woman held so many surprises.

Her small breasts fit his hands perfectly—and fit his mouth even better. He suckled at her nipples, first one then the other, until they were diamond-hard points. She moaned and gasped under his ministrations, her hands clutching at him, urging him even further.

He happily obliged. He caressed her thighs, her inner folds, pushing back his own body's demands to just take her. Tantamount to that urge was his desire to give her pleasure, all the pleasure he possibly could. Never had he felt so in control, even as his emotions spun out of control.

Her body tensed and she cried out, calling his name in her pleasure. He had never heard a sound so sweet. The pleasure he gained from hers was incredible. Nothing mattered more—except to hear the sound again and again from her.

All thoughts flew from his head when she untied his robe finally and removed it from his body.

Her hands began tormenting him, reciprocating in kind by touching him everywhere, yet never quite touching him in the most intimate of places. He tried to breathe. He could find no air. Her tiny smile hinted of triumph and more torture to come. He loved it.

She pushed him onto his back, then began to plant kisses all over his skin. She neglected no inch of him. Her lips lingered on his wound, still slightly swollen. She kissed it, as if she could take away the pain. Instead she created a more delicious one.

He throbbed. He burned. He could stand it no longer when her mouth caressed him intimately. He pulled her under him, then invaded her moist folds. She took the length of him inside herself with such perfect ease that he almost spilled his pleasure into her.

He held them both still, praying for his control to return. Her body was like fire along his own, so intimate, so incredibly Mary Ellen.

They moved together, quickly at first, desperate to sate the need driving their hearts and bodies. Then they slowed, savoring each thrust, building to exquisite satisfaction.

Her long legs wrapped around the back of his thighs, urging him farther into her. Their bodies moved in ancient rhythms that made a mockery of chemical imbalances. Peter thought he would disgrace himself and take his own pleasure without her. He gritted his teeth and held on until he heard the sweet sound of her voice crying out yet again. Only then did he surrender himself to her, vulnerable and yet unafraid.

He plunged into her one last time, spilling himself into her moistness, giving himself up to the velvet darkness surrounding them both.

MARY ELLEN WASN'T SURE how long she had been lost in the sensual storm Peter had created.

Her senses returned slowly—and with them came her common sense.

"Oh, Lordy," she muttered, pressing her hand against her forehead to hold back the jumble of emotions flooding her being.

Peter tensed, as if becoming aware of his body still intimately bound to hers. He rolled off her, lying next to her. "Mary Ellen, I don't know what came over me to be so—so animalistic."

"I think I'd actually feel better if you hadn't said that," she grumbled.

"It was the best thing I've ever felt sorry about," he offered.

She lowered her hand and glanced over at him. "Really?"

He nodded.

"Me, too." She sighed and looked back at the ceiling. Apologies were dangerous ground for them. "What have we done, Peter?"

"I don't know. Well, I do, but I can't explain my lack of restraint."

"I can't explain mine, either. I don't know what I was looking for when I came here. I only know I didn't even begin to try and stop myself. But it's worse than following an uncontrollable compulsion. We didn't use any protection for pregnancy—"

"Oh, no…you're not—"

"We don't know anything about each other's sexual health or history," she continued, determined to list all their foolishness. They'd better lay their cards on the table now, because God only knew they had laid… She didn't even want to go near that thought, she decided.

"Whoa!" he said, the blue of his eyes darkening

with worry. "I'm still coping with the first thing. Pregnancy."

"Then let's take care of the second. At least we can do that right away," she said, reaching for his robe. She put it on, and his scent immediately permeated her senses. She stripped it off and threw it over his naked middle. That solved another problem she was having at the moment. She found an end of the geometric, very male patterned coverlet. Flipping it over her body and ignoring the fainter scent of him it carried, she added, "I haven't had a relationship...encounter...for nearly a year, and my checkup last month gave me an excellent health report in all areas."

"I haven't had an encounter—" he nodded at borrowing her term "—in even longer than you and my last checkup was six months ago. It was excellent, like yours."

"Whew!" She smiled.

He smiled back, then sobered. "Do you think we made a baby?"

His voice sounded so like a scared kid's that her own panic melted away. She rolled toward him and touched his cheek. "I think we'll be okay."

From her mouth to Mother Nature's ear, she thought.

He let out his breath in a loud whoosh. "And I was worried about how this would affect the grant."

She raised herself on one elbow, not quite believing what she'd heard. "You what?"

He looked at her, his stupidity clearly dawning in his gaze. "Mary Ellen, it's not at all as it sounded."

"It isn't?" Anger nearly bubbled over inside her. Here she had been, giving her—her... She couldn't define what she'd given him, but she damn well hadn't been worried while she'd been doing so.

"What I just said was incredibly dumb and not at all what I was thinking at the time," he said, raising himself. He put his hand on her shoulder. "I thought about all the reasons we agreed upon that we shouldn't get involved with each other. And none of them mattered a damn at the time."

"Do they now?" she asked.

"Yes. For your sake. Not for mine."

Okay, so he felt exactly the same way she did. She hated it when that happened. She flopped back onto the bed. "What a mess we've made."

He flopped back with her. "Agreed. I've never seen a chemical imbalance rule so aggressively, let alone to the clinician."

"Stop talking grant talk. It turns me on."

"Sorry." He looked sheepish. "You know what I mean."

She nodded. "My Cupid theory is looking more and more viable. In fact, your wound is looking a little heart shaped."

"Don't be ridic—" He paused and looked at it. The scar did narrow to a point. "It's the way they stitched it. Besides, Roman mythology has no basis in physical reaction."

"Okay. So it's lust we're experiencing. Major lust. We're satisfied now." She gazed at him. "Aren't we?"

He swallowed visibly. "Sure."

They were both silent for a moment.

"You want to call us liars or shall I?" she asked.

"We'll both do it."

"Liar," they said together.

Peter took her hand and held it, just held it. Mary Ellen couldn't think of a nicer, more poignant gesture.

"We can't do this again."

"I know."

"We know all the reasons why."

"We do."

"We'll face the consequences of this one, should it come to that, together."

"Yes, we will."

He gripped her fingers tightly. "You *will* tell me."

"I promise."

"Good."

They lay together quietly, holding hands.

"The last time we made an agreement, this happened," she reminded him.

"Maybe we should give up agreements and apologies. They keep getting us into trouble."

They lay together for a little longer. It was nice. *Too nice,* Mary Ellen thought. Somewhere in her gut, she had regrets. Lots of them, but she wasn't ready to deal with them yet. Not when Peter was tender and emotional. Maybe she had come searching for this tonight. God, but he had such promise as a lover. If only he could just see the good side of love.

She cleared her throat. "I better go."

"Do you have to?"

She looked at him pointedly.

"Oh."

Okay, she thought. She had said all the right things. And the last thing she wanted was to go. No sooner had she said it than she knew she couldn't follow through. *Again.*

"Would you..." He stopped, then began again. "Would you stay with me tonight? Nothing will happen. I give you my word. I just don't want you to leave yet."

Peter Holiday—Mr. "It's a chemical imbalance"—

wanted her companionship, despite all the emotional dangers. Mary Ellen couldn't remember being so touched in her life by a man's need. She had always been impulsive, but he had her breaking even more rules.

"Yes. I'll stay."

He put his arm around her shoulders. They lay snuggled together for the rest of the night.

Just lay together and slept.

THE LIGHT OF DAY BROUGHT no relief. In fact, Peter found the regret list growing even longer.

"Who could have predicted my own imbalance would be so out of control?" he muttered while Mary Ellen was in his bathroom.

He found himself looking around his bedroom at the austere black-and-chrome furnishings, the white walls. He wondered what Mary Ellen thought of his decor.

Too stark, probably. Like him. Looking back on his life, he realized he had spent too few hours in his home, preferring the lab and the classroom. He even disliked making a home, really. He'd often bragged that he needed only a bed and a refrigerator to get by. Now he had nothing to show in his personal life—except a very lonely existence. He could talk a lot about eliminating emotions, yet what he had in their place wasn't much.

She emerged from the bathroom, wearing the same clothes in which she had arrived last night. Her hair, turned a deep auburn by her shower, clung in damp, silken ropes to her shoulders. She had never looked more beautiful. He wanted to make love with her again. Right now. And then again after that....

Peter gazed at her abdomen. He wondered if she

were pregnant. The thought scared him silly—and yet it didn't.

"Hi," he said, smiling.

She smiled back. "Hi, yourself. Do you have anything for breakfast? I'm starved."

He laughed, delighted with her mundane request. "I have everything. I believe in a good breakfast."

"Me, too." She wrinkled her nose. "We've got to stop being compatible like this."

"Why?"

She gave him that "wake up and smell the coffee" look.

"Oh."

He dressed and followed her downstairs. They moved easily together in his kitchen while fixing breakfast. Another compatibility, he thought. After the initial tucking in of cereal, rye toast and fruit, he said, "I'm really proud of us. We just slept together. I hadn't realized how comforting that could be."

"We had good incentive to *only* sleep," she reminded him with a wry grin.

"That's true...but let's not diminish the achievement."

"Agreed." She sipped juice, then said, "Peter, I know I was angry with you over the grant thing last night, but you were right to have qualms about it."

"No," he began.

"Yes." She shook her head. "I don't know what's going on between us, but it's got to stop for your sake. My father is a generous man, but he's very rigid sometimes."

Peter reached across the table to take her hand. "I'm not worried about your father, Mary Ellen."

"Well, you should be." Her momentary emotions

shifted. "He also has a sense of morality. If he thought we were having a relationship, he wouldn't give you the grant because he'd risk accusations of favoritism. I know him and I know he wouldn't want the foundation tainted. He wouldn't tolerate even a wisp of that. He wouldn't care how good your research might be or how much people would need it. That's what I mean by rigid. He won't be budged once he makes a decision, and if he makes it against you, he won't change his mind."

"I'm not worried," Peter repeated, although his stomach churned.

She gripped his fingers tightly. "Do I have to hit you over the head with a two-by-four to get this into your skull? I've always been impulsive, but I can't allow you to pay for my impulsiveness this time. You were right about this having to stop, especially now. I thought a lot in the shower and it's time I grew up."

Peter stared at her, surprised by her stance and oddly hurt. "I've got to keep you out of the bathroom."

Her eyes teared up again, and she gave a watery chuckle. She patted the back of his hand with her free one. "Oh, Peter, don't ever change."

He didn't know why she would say that. He wasn't sure what she found to her liking, but he was grateful she did. Still, he was sure she was wrong. "I can't believe you're talking like this. It's so...sensible!"

"I told you I grew up in the bathroom."

"Well, I don't like it." He squeezed her fingers. "Let me take care of me."

"Peter, if I have the sense of a pea pod, you're in even worse shape. At least I'm not naive."

"I'm not naive!"

"Of course you are. Why else would you think love is a chemical imbalance?"

"I'm very close to proving it, definitively," he said, annoyed that she thought he was naive. She, not being a scientist, didn't understand the body's workings. She would, when he proved his theory right. But he wasn't naive.

"Save the debate for the grant people, and I'll save you for them," she told him.

"No," he replied, disturbed that he wouldn't see her again when all he wanted to do was to make love to her. "I want to see you again, Mary Ellen."

"I shot you in the butt with an arrow," she reminded him.

"So you're exciting beyond words."

"I got you in trouble once with my father."

"I won't be run off because of that."

"I'm impulsive."

"I study impulsive behavior."

"Do you hear yourself?" she asked. "You sound like me. I'm already having a bad influence on you."

He was about to disagree, but clamped his lips shut. Maybe she was right about bad influences. He couldn't understand why he was arguing to continue to see her. Yet it bothered him to just walk away because of complications. Never before had he felt so many things for a woman. His biochemicals must be running amok, but the exhilaration was incredible. He wasn't ready to give up the feeling just yet.

Or maybe underneath her nobility, she was trying to let him down easy. Maybe he had been lacking in the bedroom. She had *seemed* enthusiastic. In fact, she had done that one thing with her tongue....

Women were known to fake their physical responses. Maybe he really was naive. "I was a failure last night, wasn't I? You're trying to kiss me off because I'm no Don Juan."

"Peter!" She laughed and cried at the same time. Gripping both his hands tightly, she said, "Listen up, stud muffin. You were fantastic last night and I want nothing more than for you to keep making love to me until I die a happy woman. Which won't be long. Not the way you do it."

"Really?"

"Honest."

"I am a stud muffin?"

"The best-kept male secret since Brad Pitt."

"*Thelma and Louise*? *A River Runs Through It*? Or *Legends of the Fall*?"

"*Legends.*"

He grinned widely. "You can be my Julia Ormond anytime you want."

She chuckled and shook her head. "God, the male ego. See how naive you are? You don't even know your own sex appeal."

"Maybe I needed the right person to bring it out in me. By the way, will flattery get me anywhere?"

"Peter, please. Get serious." She glanced around the kitchen. "I can't believe I just said that."

"Me, neither."

"Peter, really. We can't see each other like this anymore."

That strange compulsion that had held him in sway since the moment he had met her now returned tenfold. He could *not* let her go.

"No," he said.

"Yes."

"I won't allow it."

Mary Ellen laughed. "Peter, you can't just say that and expect to be obeyed."

"Why not? Or do you really not want to see me anymore?"

She sobered. "I want to see you more than anything else on this earth. Honest."

"So do I. Honest."

"Naive boy."

"All right, then if you're being logical—and I can't believe you even know what it is—"

She sniffed indignantly. "Thanks a lot."

"You're welcome. But if you're on this logical bent, then let's truly be logical about this. We have this compulsion to be together, right?"

"An understatement, but yes."

"We've tried to fight it, but we've been unsuccessful."

"Understatement number two, but yes again."

"Now. I will lose the grant if we continue to see each other."

"Yes. My father will withdraw from you, and I cannot allow that to happen."

"So you insist on being noble."

"Logical. But absolutely. I might have shot you on Valentine's Day, but that's no excuse."

He smiled. "I could withdraw my research from grant consideration and neatly solve this."

"You know you can't. The moment you withdraw from the Magnussen Foundation grant, other foundations will never take your application seriously. Unless you show something is wrong with the Magnussen Foundation. Which there isn't, so no one will believe you. That would only make you look even more unreliable. Besides, doesn't your research center depend on grant money?"

"You *are* being logical," he said in awe. He straightened. "Despite what you say, withdrawing is an option. A drastic one, I admit, but it can be done without dire consequences. I've seen centers weather withdrawals from prestigious grants and not get burned for all time. It is a possibility."

"No, it's not. Not for you or for me. Don't even try it." Her chin quivered. "See? Mine is the only option, Peter. Try to understand—"

"You've missed another alternative."

Her jaw dropped. "I have?"

"We could hold off seeing each other until the grant is formally awarded. Then there would be no question of collusion, favoritism or anything else to taint the process."

Mary Ellen swept their breakfast dishes aside, crawled onto the table and hugged him. She punctuated kisses with words. "You're so wonderful! Brilliant! Terrific!"

"Next time, leave the logic to those who can deal with it." He grinned happily while she continued to kiss his cheeks and forehead. She could keep doing that forever as far as he was concerned. Several ideas entered his head about a certain movie with a certain breakfast lovemaking scene. Hell, they had the table half-cleared already....

Mary Ellen let him go and eyed him sourly. "Don't play smart mouth without a full deck, honey."

He had to smile at her. It was nice to be the smart mouth for once, half a deck or not. He brushed the hair back from her face. "I might have suggested a postponement, but I don't want to agree to it, Mary Ellen."

"But we will." Her voice was firm. "Peter, I have to. For you."

She kissed his lips, tenderly at first and then with growing passion. Their tongues met. Peter tasted her sweetness and wanted nothing more than to take advantage of the table.

"I want you," he whispered, his hands on her breasts.

"Not as much as I want you."

"More." He eased her away from him. "I put you at risk once. I won't do it again."

"We'll be all right...." she began, her fingers clutching at his shirt.

"No. It's my turn to be noble."

"Oh, Peter."

She looked as if she would melt. He liked the notion that he could put her in that state. "We'll wait."

She coughed. "Our track record's not too good about that."

"You're the one who wants to be *too* noble!"

"We've established that logical thinking is not my forte." She glanced at her watch. "Hell, I'm late for work."

Peter turned her wrist and looked at her watch, too. "Hell, I'm *very* late for work."

"I guess that's killed the mood." She crawled off the table and began to pick up their dishes. She paused. "We can call each other, can't we?"

"We'd better," he said, liking the idea.

"We can do this, can't we?"

"Yes. I think these...urgings we can't seem to fight have got to run their course."

"I don't like the sound of that."

"I'm only being logical."

"But emotions aren't logical. Remember, that's why you want to cure them."

"I know that."

"Why don't you want to cure us?"

His mouth opened. No words emerged. He shut it, took a breath and tried again. "We're in lust."

She grinned. "I like that."

"Me, too." Already he didn't like the delay in their coming together again, but he accepted it more readily than anything else they'd tried so far. At least his insides didn't churn with that overwhelming compulsion. This time he could control himself and his reaction to her. He just wished he understood it.

Despite everything, he liked her. She made him laugh. She made him feel good. She challenged him in ways he'd never thought about. He wanted to explore them. As he had told her, he wanted to allow their urgings to run their course wherever they might lead. And realistically, he couldn't turn away from her. Not yet. His father said don't marry for love. His grandparents had showed him the wisdom of that. He and Mary Ellen had many things in common—and maybe the beginnings of a passionate friendship. That could count for a lot.

He nearly didn't control his reactions when he kissed her goodbye a short time later.

"Peter, could we...?" she began, pressing herself suggestively against him.

"Dammit, Mary Ellen. You would tempt *Saint* Peter," he said, even as he tightened his arms around her.

"As long as I tempt you. The university's holding a reception for my father when he gets back from Scotland," she said. "He donated a library wing. Did you get invited?"

"Yes." He grinned. "We'd be able to see each other there."

"As long as we behave," she reminded him.

They parted, with the promise to call each other later.

They could do this, Peter told himself while he watched her get in her car and drive away.

They could.

He walked back into the kitchen and spotted his doughnut ring lying discarded on a chair. He hadn't even missed it this morning, he thought. Or last night.

With a grin, he picked it up and went out the back door. Happily, he flung it like a Frisbee. One cure down. One to go.

He wondered how eager he was for the second.

Chapter Five

Mary Ellen anxiously searched the crowded ballroom floor, looking through the sea of faces for one in particular.

Two weeks.

She and Peter had talked on the telephone every day, several times a day, but they hadn't seen each other in that time. They hadn't touched, although they had begun to know more about each other. She knew his parents lived in Rumson, New Jersey. She liked that name. He knew her mother never left her Palm Beach home. They had discovered more compatible likes and dislikes, including liver in the yuck category and chocolate milk in the yum one.

This phone arrangement, better than a complete break, still stank to high heavens, yet she refused to follow her impulse to see him. She would be mature. Peter's livelihood depended on it. Unfortunately, his livelihood bothered her more and more.

She put the thought out of her head, determined to enjoy the evening. Tonight's reception was a risk-free time to see Peter. A freebie. Thank goodness her father had donated the funds for a new wing to the University of Pennsylvania library. Thank goodness as well that the university had decided to celebrate the donation. Now she could see Peter. All the grant candidates had been invited.

"You look lovely tonight."

Surprised by the voice in her ear, Mary Ellen turned. Even as she did, she knew who was at her side.

"Hello, Jeremy," she said. "Thank you for the lovely compliment."

"You're more than welcome."

His gaze raked her bare shoulders and bosom swelling over the strapless mauve gown. Mary Ellen didn't feel a single physical response. A slight disgust, maybe, but Jeremy's leer was more pathetic than threatening.

"Would you like to dance?" he asked.

Mary Ellen maintained her smile while she thought like lightning. She didn't want to dance with Jeremy. Who would? On the other hand, the dance floor afforded her a better view of the crowd. From there she might find Peter more easily than from here. She held out her hand. "Thanks. I'd enjoy dancing right now."

No lie, at least.

Jeremy danced smoothly enough, although he had a tendency to turn her hard to the right during the old-fashioned waltz.

"This is wonderful for your father," Jeremy said, smiling and nodding his head in agreement with himself. "He's been such a friend to education. With our funding coming more and more from the private sector, we're grateful to have men like your father, who understand that without academia, we would have nothing."

"He's great," Mary Ellen said absently. The groups of people standing on the sidelines and around the buffet table held her attention. Unfortunately, the damn dancers kept sweeping by, blocking her view.

"My own research needs a man of your father's stature to understand its significance. The tree frog's existence is really the basis for the ecosystem of the rain forest. We must keep it safe."

She gazed around, trying to spot Peter. It was impossible for her to recognize people when she was spinning like this. "Have you seen Peter here yet? Dr. Holiday, I mean."

Jeremy stumbled slightly, then recovered. "No. Why?"

"Just wondering."

All of a sudden, the crowd parted like the Red Sea to reveal Peter standing by the entryway.

Mary Ellen grinned, relieved to have found him. Then she realized she couldn't leave in the middle of the dance and rush over to him. She sobered. This new restraint was killing her. "Hell."

"I beg your pardon?"

"Nothing." She forced herself to smile even as she wondered when the damnable song would end. Finally, it did. "That was lovely, Jeremy. Thank you."

"About the tree frog—"

"Oh, my, look at the time." She tapped her watch without glancing at it. "Cinderella and all that. I've got to go."

She strode away, while muttering, "Cinderella? Oh, man. Even Dopey could do better."

She would apologize to Jeremy later for her rudeness. Right now she had more important things to take care of.

Something warned her not to run straight to Peter. She caught sight of her father chatting with some of his friends. He was facing her even though he didn't look directly at her. She couldn't take a chance that he might eventually.

She grabbed up a champagne glass from a passing waiter, who protested that the glass was empty and needed to be cleaned.

"I'm not thirsty," she assured him, before moving away.

She mingled and chatted, waving her empty glass for emphasis and all the while purposefully making her way toward the object of her lust. For lust she did.

Peter's shoulders looked broader and his waist narrower in the tuxedo he wore. She knew what those shoulders felt like under her hands. His skin would be hot, his muscles lean like a tennis player's. She loved the way they moved when he was inside her. Peter, in his honest, raw responses, had left her with a hunger that would last forever. The past weeks had been more than forever. Forever in hell was more like it.

She remembered their conversation of three days ago, when she'd told him she wasn't pregnant. He had been silent for a long moment, then sounded relieved. She knew his feelings had been as mixed as her own. *How odd,* she thought. She had always been so careful before in relationships. If she didn't know better, she'd think she regretted *not* paying the consequences.

She slipped in beside him, feeling strangely shy. He had been loading his plate with pot stickers and shrimp. Disappointment shot through her that he hadn't lost his appetite over their enforced separation.

"Peter," she said in a low voice.

The plate wobbled most satisfactorily, as she took him by surprise. She liked that she could. His gazed turned to her. She held her breath. A myriad of emotions lay open for her in those baby blues. Excitement. Hesitation. Regret. Desire. He hid nothing. His hunger for her clearly said no amount of food would appease it.

"How the hell is that dress staying up?" he asked. "It's against the laws of physics."

"As long as I hold my breath, it's okay," she said.

"Do you have to be half-naked?" he asked, staring at her breasts. "All the men are looking at you. I hate it."

She laughed happily. "No one's looking at me except you. I like that."

"The men damn well better not be," he muttered, shoving a shrimp in his mouth. His gaze softened. "God, but you look sensational. I've missed you."

She swallowed. "Oh, Peter. I've missed you, too."

"The phone calls are not enough."

He was weakening. She couldn't allow that. She would have to be the strong one. She tightened her resolve. "We'll survive on the calls. And the chance meetings like this. We have to."

"Are you always this stubborn?" he asked.

"Only when it matters. You're backing up the line," she added sensibly.

Peter looked beyond her to the restless line of people. He moved through the buffet in record time, bypassing nearly everything. Mary Ellen followed dutifully behind him. She took nothing. Her hunger demanded only one thing: him.

She knew she really shouldn't stay overly long with him, not if she didn't want to arouse any suspicions. Still, she wouldn't leave him right after she'd found him. Not just yet.

They no sooner located a vacated table in the anteroom when Peter looked at his plate. "Why did I take all this food?"

"I haven't a clue." The shrimp looked good, however, and the pot stickers even better. She picked one up and ate it. The minced pork and ginger ignited her senses. She reached for another.

Peter smiled. "I think I know why now."

Before she could reply, two young women stopped at their table. From their long, shining hair and fresh, peaches-and-cream complexions, they were obviously students.

"Dr. Holiday, we just had to tell you how much we enjoyed your guest lecture last month at our anthropology class," one said. Both giggled. "It was like…awesome."

"Thank you." Peter looked too damned pleased, to Mary Ellen's mind. "I'm so glad you enjoyed it. I see more kids asleep, usually, in my audiences—"

"Oh, not us. We were just fascinated."

Mary Ellen bet they were fascinated. They looked like a couple of she-wolves with a victim in their sights.

The girls glanced at each other, then back to Peter. "We'd love to be part of your studies. Or as research volunteers for your center. Do you need volunteers or assistants? We could really help you. And it would help our college records, too."

"Well…"

Mary Ellen fumed at his hesitation.

"Call the research center tomorrow and see what we might have," he said finally.

"Oh, thank you, Doctor. You're awesome!"

They left, giggling like maddened hyenas.

Mary Ellen snorted. "Do you believe that? They

may as well have hung signs on their chests proclaiming they're hot for the sexy doctor. I'm surprised they didn't write Love You on their eyelids, then flutter them like crazy until you got the message."

Peter turned and looked after the girls. "You really think they have a crush on me?"

"Like you're Indiana Jones." She sighed and shook her head at him. "You would buy the Brooklyn Bridge, I think."

"Why do you insist I'm so naive?"

"It's part of your charm. And don't look so smug about those girls, either."

He smiled. "I have to admit I like your annoyance."

"I'll be an annoyance all over you, if you get any ideas about those two."

"Too young," he told her crisply. "Besides, I would never get involved with a student. It's always struck me as being predatory, and what would I have in common with some kid?"

"Keep that in mind."

He chuckled. "I will."

She let out her breath, pleased with his common sense about sweet young things. "I wish we could run away from here and—"

"Don't tempt me." He drew in a ragged breath. "We could dance."

"Can you?" she asked curiously.

"Yes. I keep telling you I'm not a total geek."

"I know it better than most."

They gazed at each other. All kinds of physical sensations swirled through her. She couldn't touch him. She couldn't.

His foot did accidentally touch hers under the table. She realized the tablecloth's skirt hid the movement.

Unable to resist, she stretched her foot out, caressing his calf with the side of her high heel.

Peter stilled, wide-eyed. "Mary Ellen."

"What?" She smiled innocently. Inside, she felt anything but innocent. The silk of his trousers against the silk of her hose made her feel incredibly sexy. His consternation only heightened her senses. She raised her foot higher....

Let's see him control this response, she thought.

"Mary Ellen!" he said through gritted teeth, when her foot traveled dangerously high along the inside of his thigh.

He grabbed her ankle, clearly intending to stop her. But his warm grip sent her breath hissing sharply from her lungs. His fingers held her leg still, then slowly moved up her calf. Far too slowly. Her blood heated. He massaged her muscle, turning her insides to mush. He was no innocent. His emotions might be raw and unfettered, but his hand had gained much experience about her body.

His fingers crept up farther, to her thigh. A tiny moan escaped from the back of her throat.

"Here you are, girl."

Her father's voice was a cold dash of water over her growing heat. She blinked. Peter pushed her foot away as if it suddenly burned him.

Only her foot didn't drop to the floor.

"Dad," Mary Ellen said by way of greeting, while trying to free her thin heel from where it had caught in a fold of Peter's pant leg.

Peter glanced at her, panic in his eyes. He cleared his throat. "This is a wonderful reception, Mr. Magnussen. The university really went all out to thank you for the wing."

Without standing up, he offered his hand, the same hand that had just caressed her thigh, to her father.

What a man, Mary Ellen thought, awed by the courage behind the politeness.

"I'm paying them enough," her father grumbled, shaking Peter's hand.

Taking advantage of her father's diverted attention, she tugged at her foot, trying to free it. Instead, she felt the tiniest of rips. Peter's panicked look doubled. *Hell,* she thought. She couldn't free her shoe without tearing his trousers from him. As tempting as that might be, the reception was hardly the place for it. She let her foot hang.

"Dad, stop sounding like they twisted your arm or held a gun to your head. You loved doing it."

Her father grimaced. "Okay. But I didn't expect this big bash. Hell, I'm only a believer in the value of education and research."

"We know." She reached out and patted her father's arm. He was hard and harsh at times, demanding of others as much as he demanded of himself. He hated his soft spots to show and they rarely did. Sometimes with her, when they were alone, but that was all.

"How about a dance with the old man?"

Oh boy, Mary Ellen thought. If life could go wrong, it would. For one brief moment, she wondered how her father would react to being informed his daughter's game of footsie was still in progress. Not well, she bet. Rather than tempt fate, she said, "Anytime, Dad. How about if I catch up with you right after I've finished my little snack here with Peter and freshen up?"

"Sure." Her father glanced from one to the other, his look clearly speculative. "You remember what I said before?"

She waved a hand. "Oh, sure. Not to worry."

Her father looked at them once more, then left.

"That was close," she muttered, reaching under the table to flip off her shoe. The moment the weight of her foot was removed, her shoe came free of his pant leg. It figured.

Peter flopped back in his chair. "I thought I would have a heart attack when he asked you to dance."

"I thought we were dead meat long before that." She grinned. "When you play footsie, you don't fool around."

"Thank you." He grew serious. "I can't stand this. I want to be with you. Alone."

"Oh, Peter," she murmured, feeling exactly the same way. They had just averted disaster and he wanted to start it all over again. And she wanted nothing more than to help him.

"I suppose you better go dance with your father. I suppose I can handle that."

"You should dance with some women," she advised him. She added quickly, "*Not* sweet, young, horny students with crushes on you. Find a couple of blue-haired matrons with droopy bosoms."

"I'm certainly looking forward to that." He eyed her. "You better do the same."

"Peter, I think I would attract a great deal of attention if I danced with blue-haired, droopy-bosomed matrons."

"Why?"

She just laughed. She liked him playful like this. She liked the way his white, white shirt accented his square jaw, dark hair and blue eyes. She liked the bow tie, too. In fact, she liked the way he looked in formal clothes and what it did to her far too much. Why did he have to be such a nonbeliever in the benefits of human emotion?

They rose together from their cozy table. She didn't suggest they dance together. Neither did he. They couldn't take the closeness of their bodies, their arms around each other. They would be stripping their clothes off and giving mating lessons instead. No amount of chemical imbalances could explain that to her father. On the other hand, it might drive him to fund Peter's research, just to avoid the embarrassment again.

"Meet me later," Peter said. "After we dance with the blue hairs."

"We shouldn't." She wished the words back. They sounded far too tentative.

"I know we shouldn't. That's why we have to. One time. Just for a kiss. Who knows when we'll have another chance like this?"

He would tempt an angel, she thought. She would have to be stronger than one.

"Maybe."

PETER WATCHED MARY ELLEN dance with her father. He watched her dance with several other men. Even though she stuck to the male version of the "blue hairs," it didn't help his growing foul mood.

She looked too damned beautiful, for one thing. She had pulled her very auburn hair into an intricate knot at the nape of her neck. He itched to free the dark red strands and let them wind around his fingers. He wanted to kiss those creamy shoulders until she cried out with need for him. He wanted to strip that clinging, gossamer gown from her body and make love to her until he died of happiness. Just as she had said the last time they'd been together.

Seeing her now only reminded him that these last two weeks had been the worst of his entire life.

He had lived for the nightly phone calls. He hadn't thought the wanting could get worse, but it had. Tonight proved that. Actually having her in the same room and not being able to give in to the least impulse was sheer torture. He had tasted heaven and been plunged into hell, and he would not put up with it any longer.

He must be crazy because…he had a plan.

He picked another matron to dance with him. As the soundtrack from *Saturday Night Fever* played, he boogied with his partner in Mary Ellen's general direction. Soon he was back-to-back with her.

"Turn around," he muttered, doing a slow spin.

She didn't.

"Turn around!" he said louder, hoping she could hear him now over the music.

"Oh." She gracefully spun around, but too fast to be in sync with him.

Peter cursed under his breath when he faced his real partner once more. He tried again. "Slower!"

"What?" His partner cupped her ear, waving one hand at the loud music and voices surrounding them.

"Now!" Mary Ellen said, forestalling his reply.

Peter shrugged at his partner, then turned. He met Mary Ellen's gaze. Finally. "Perfect! Meet me. I've found a place."

He wiggled the rest of the way around his little spin. This was fun, he thought. His heart pounded with anticipation and his blood rushed enthusiastically through his veins. Was this what humans felt in a truly passionate relationship? No wonder people went nuts when they lost the feeling. Something could be said for impulsive behavior.

"Who are you?" his partner asked.

"Dr. Peter Holiday." He felt a hand slap his back as if by accident. "One moment."

He made his turn on cue.

"Are you crazy?" Mary Ellen exclaimed, waving her hips deliciously in time to the music.

He chuckled. "I hope not."

The music stopped before he could tell her what time to meet him. They turned back to their respective partners, having no other choice. He thanked his partner, who turned out to be the retired dean of admissions' wife. The sweet lady had no clue she had been his cover. He glanced back to find Mary Ellen had already departed in the opposite direction.

He casually made his way along the edge of the ballroom until he stood behind her again. She was with a small group of people she obviously knew. He didn't recognize a single one, not that it mattered. Clearly, for someone who worked in the sports world, she was as comfortable as her father at academia socializing.

He looked around, again casually, determining that her father was far away and occupied. No one else seemed interested in him. He leaned forward and whispered into her hair. "Two doors past the ladies' room. Ten forty-five."

Mary Ellen coughed. Actually, it sounded as though she was choking.

Peter frowned. Was her cough a yes or a no? He couldn't tell. Whispering, he said, "Cough once for yes and twice for no."

She coughed twice.

"Ah. I knew you meant yes." He wasn't taking no for an answer, after all. Nobility only went so far.

She coughed twice again.

"Can I get you a drink of water?" Peter asked in a loud voice, playing a concerned passerby.

Mary Ellen glared at him.

"Are you sure?" He didn't wait for a reply. "What time do you have?"

She blinked, caught off guard, then glanced at her watch. "Ten-thirty."

"Exactly?"

"Well..." She glanced again. "Ten thirty-two."

He adjusted his watch to match hers, then looked at her pointedly, sending the obvious message. "Take care of that cough, miss."

"Oh, I will." She looked daggers at him.

If nothing else, she'd show up just to murder him, Peter thought in amusement. Either way, his mission would be accomplished.

He went to the small, empty coatroom he'd discovered earlier on a trip to the men's room. At the end of the hall, off the front lobby, the room ensured no one would see them together. The hallway had been deserted when he had come through before. Mary Ellen had a better excuse, with the ladies' room close by the coatroom. The men's room was on the other side of the hall.

Alone and impatiently waiting, he felt his stomach churn. Would she come to him? What if she didn't? What the hell was he doing?

The woman had shot him with an arrow, causing great humiliation. He had made love to her against his better judgment. He was still risking his livelihood just to kiss her one more time. His common sense was shot to kingdom come. Why? Why was he doing this? He couldn't give the least explanation—except for Mary Ellen herself. He was so drawn to her, it was as if the arrow was connected between them. Something was connected between them, for he couldn't resist being with her for a few stolen moments no matter what he risked.

He should leave right now. He put his hand on the doorknob, fighting for his willpower, trying to make himself banish this madness. His fingers refused to turn the knob. His cure for impulsive emotional behavior was almost ready for human consumption. At this rate, he'd be his first patient.

What was it about Mary Ellen that had him acting so out of control? Was it the aura of excitement that surrounded her? The way she moved? The kisses that pushed him over the edge? The unique taste of her?

The doorknob turned under his fingers. After a frozen moment, he realized he wasn't the one turning it. He stepped back as the door opened, bracing himself for some innocent way to explain his presence in the coatroom. Looking for a lost comb probably wouldn't cut it.

"You are a crazy man!" Mary Ellen said, coming into the room and slamming the door behind her.

He pulled her to him, feeling the shock of her body against his right down to his toes. Her perfume filled his senses, enticing him to be wild and free. His mouth found hers, pressing it open for his kiss. His tongue darted in, claiming her own, tasting her sweetness. Her arms went around his neck tightly, her fingers gripping his hair. He cupped her bottom, loving the way her curves fit his hands. His need grew. One kiss would never satisfy him. Never.

When his mouth finally did ease from hers, she put a hand to her head as if she were dizzy and about to faint. "Peter, you're insane."

"For you," he admitted. The upper globes of her breasts, swelling above the precarious bodice, intrigued him. "How do they do that?"

She giggled. "Magic."

"Really?" He crooked a finger in the center of the bodice and tugged. The top of the gown fell away from her breasts, leaving them splendidly bare. "It *is* magic!"

Her nipples were already puckered from her reaction to the kiss. He cupped her breast, watching the way his fingers curved completely around them. He bent down and sucked hard on one nipple, feeling the point distend in his mouth. Mary Ellen moaned, clutching his hair, guiding his lips and tongue. He lifted her long skirt, the flimsy material slipping in his palms. Her legs were pure silk from her hose. His hand glided along her flesh. He encountered a lacy panty. His brain raged with images—of her naked beneath him...her woman's flesh enclosing him in ecstasy...their thrusting together harder and faster....

"Peter." Slowly, Mary Ellen disentangled herself from his embrace. She pulled up her dress front. "We can't do this. We have to stop now."

He could hear his own breath whistling in his lungs. "You're right. I know you're right."

Voices penetrated his scrambled mind. He stilled. Mary Ellen gave a tiny squeak of protest. His ragged breath mingled with hers, the only sound in the tiny room.

"In here?" a querulous tone asked.

"No, Mother. I told you the ladies' room is back here."

"I can't see a thing. The light's terrible. You'd think the hotel would have better lighting."

"If you wore your glasses, Mother—"

"I don't need them!"

The voices faded down the hall. The faint whoosh of a heavy-duty door pump penetrated the coatroom.

Peter took a deep breath, trying to calm the adrenaline shooting through his body. "That was close."

"You are the master of understatement." She gazed at him. "What am I going to do with you?"

He shrugged. "I don't know."

"Me, neither. This is dangerous, meeting like this, let alone—" She interrupted herself. "If those two women hadn't come along, I'm afraid of what would have happened. It might not have been just one kiss, Peter."

He wondered if he should point out that was a song from *Bye Bye Birdie*, then decided against it. She wasn't in a movie mood at the moment. "Well, we did keep it to one kiss."

"And a major grope!"

He grinned. He couldn't help it.

"Peter, how am I suppose to save you when you won't cooperate?"

"I told you. You don't need to save me."

"I swear, I really am a bad influence on you. You're turning into me!"

"Are you saying you didn't want to be here?" he asked.

"No! Oh, no." She touched his cheek before wearily leaning against the wall. "I couldn't stay away. I admit it. Especially with you creeping around playing I Spy and endearing yourself at every turn.''

He endeared himself to her. He liked the sound of it. But he saw her dilemma. Truly, it was his own as well. "Granted, we got carried away tonight, but we haven't seen each other in weeks. What did you expect?''

"I don't know. You're like a drug and I can't stay away from you.''

He felt the same about her. His behavior in her presence was absolutely unexplainable, and he didn't care. He just wanted to be with her. This—this high...was that what people went so crazy to have and not lose? Suddenly, he understood the insanity, and he couldn't imagine eliminating the giddy sensations.

"I have to go," she said.

He put his hands on her shoulders to stop her. "Mary Ellen—''

She ducked out of his embrace. "No. Now that's enough. Another kiss and God knows what I'll do next.''

"I like the sound of that.''

"Me, too. Too well.'' She opened the coatroom door a bare inch and peeked out. "The coast is clear.''

He caught her hand just as she slipped through the door. He kissed her fingers. "Call me tonight.''

She was gone.

Peter waited a few more minutes, then checked the hallway. Finding it empty, he emerged from their rendezvous place.

Jeremy Chelios turned the corner at the opposite end of the hall. At the same moment, Mary Ellen came out of the ladies'-room door.

All three of them stopped and stared at one another.

"Good evening," Mary Ellen said, nodding and walking blithely past Jeremy.

Boy, she was good, Peter thought. Unfortunately, she left him to cope with his rival. Peter would make her pay later. Much later.

He decided to take another page from Mary Ellen's book. He sauntered toward Jeremy. When he got close enough, he said, "Evening, Chelios."

"What were you doing with Mary Ellen?" Jeremy demanded.

Peter raised his eyebrows. "What the hell are you talking about? She was in the ladies' room. You saw her come out of it yourself. And you saw I didn't."

"You weren't in the men's room. That's here." Chelios pointed to the appropriate door. "On *this* side of the hallway."

"Your eyesight isn't that bad, after all. What a miracle."

"You better explain yourself, Holiday. Or do I have to go to John about this?"

"Over what?" Peter asked, with more bravado than he felt. He had to stop the man before he did such a thing. Suddenly, the grant, which Peter had been willing to risk, became important again. If he were to lose it, he preferred to do so to a worthier project rather than to some social technicality. "You're going to look like a complete fool, Jeremy, when you have to tell Magnussen that Mary Ellen and I were in separate rooms. Think about it and decide where being a ninny would put you with the grant you covet so much."

Peter realized he'd given himself a great exit line. So he took it. Stage right.

Chapter Six

The telephone rang right on time.

Mary Ellen snatched up the receiver from its cradle in her eagerness to hear Peter's voice.

"Hello?" she asked breathlessly.

"It's me."

She relaxed back in her bed at the familiar baritone. "Have I ever told you that you have a sexy voice?"

"Not yet. So do you. I won't be responsible for what happens if you sing me 'Happy Birthday, Mr. President.'"

She giggled like a schoolgirl. She felt like one with her first crush. "You realize this is all we're reduced to again. Phone sex."

"I'm miserable...and then again I'm not. What are you wearing?"

She smothered another giggle. He sounded just like his cousin, Raymond, the city's premier sports-talk radio host, when he flirted with listeners. That had been a bit of extra information from this round of phone calls. Michael, another of the cousins Peter mentioned, was a nationally syndicated columnist and Jared, the third, was a well-known divorce lawyer. Who'd have thought it? She wouldn't have, not from her Mr. Innocent.

She looked down at herself. She loved these daily good-night calls. "I'm not wearing a thing."

His breath hissed over the phone line. "Honest?"

"Mmm." She deliberately kept her murmur noncommittal. Let it drive him crazy. "What are *you* wearing?"

"Too much."

She laughed. Then she sighed. "I miss you."

"I miss you, too."

The reception had been ages ago, and they'd been together only that one time in weeks. One time! The temptation to drive to his house or office at any given moment nearly overwhelmed her on occasion. She hung in there, clinging to her newfound pride and control like lifelines. She *was* proud of herself for learning restraint. She hated herself, too, for it. Something had to give soon. Like her father and the grant.

"Why does it have to be the end of April for a decision on that turkey grant?" she asked. Peter had told her earlier of the new date he'd been given for the symposium.

"I told you, schedules were a problem and one of the committee members had to have surgery. He can't get out much until then. We must be patient. It's not that long. What—six weeks? Frankly, I could use the time to prepare my presentation."

"I suppose that's not much." She wouldn't survive longer on these calls. That she'd made it this far boggled her mind. She tried to reassure herself that the phone calls were still coming and that was a good sign for them. But she knew her limits and she had just about reached them.

"We'll make it until then," Peter said.

"You always say that."

"We're mature adults."

"You always say that, too." She sighed. "I'm being grumpy. I'm sorry. I think I'm hoping you'll turn into that crazed nut again from the night of the reception."

"Jeremy, that bastard, has made me wary of a repeat."

"Maybe it's out of sight, out of mind for you," she said, voicing an overriding concern in her mind.

"Hardly." His answer came quick and sure. "I can't get you out of my head. I can barely concentrate on my work. Maybe I can control my impulsive behavior a little more. Maybe I'm a major masochist."

"I think I must be one, too." She shook her head. "It's just that you were so cute running around and whispering all sorts of instructions."

"Cute, huh?"

"Very cute."

"You don't think like most people, Mary Ellen."

"Are you complaining?"

"No."

"So we wait this out like mature adults."

"It's what we agreed to. It's what *you* insisted upon."

"I know."

She wondered why she was hanging in with him. Peter's work to eliminate romantic love showed he had no personal interest in the long-term relationship love usually brought. Yet he showed so much personal promise on the subject of commitment. He was playful and endearing, hungry only for her and not willing to accept the obstacles to a relationship in their path. Every glimpse she caught of these facets of him only whetted her appetite the more. Yet what was the end goal in all this? Not love. He would be the first to tell her that.

A notion occurred to her, one that sent her blood racing through her veins. What if she took the time until the symposium to change his mind about love? Maybe she could show him how good it could be. Maybe he would see how much humanity's ability to love had already brought it to a higher level of civilization.

Nobody wanted to show him all that more than she.

A little imp surfaced inside Mary Ellen's head. Letting her tone drop, she said, "I know I insisted upon just phone calls, but I'm lonely, Peter. And naked. And in my bed—"

"Don't start this," he warned.

"Happy birthday...to you," she crooned in her best Marilyn Monroe imitation. "Happy birthday...to you..."

"You're killing me, woman."

"Good. Happy birthday, Mr. President..."

He hung up the phone.

She set the receiver down and grinned.

The telephone rang.

When she picked it up, Peter said, "That was rotten."

"I know. Shall I sing it again?"

"Yes. I'm already naked and waiting."

She laughed.

"In fact..." He proceeded to describe to her in great detail what he would do if he were in her bed right then.

Mary Ellen swallowed. Her face held a rosy heat.

Her blood throbbed. She could only quote Susan Sarandon in *Bull Durham*. "Oh, my!"

"I'll call you tomorrow," Peter said.

The line clicked and went dead.

Stunned, Mary Ellen stared at the phone for a minute. Then she laughed. He had learned playfulness too well. Peter Holiday was becoming full of surprises.

That thought ran through her head during dinner with her father later in the week.

"I've got a meeting in an hour," he announced, the moment he sat down at the table. He'd been late as it was, coming in the door just a few minutes ago.

Mary Ellen lifted an eyebrow. "Wow! A whole hour. Good thing we're having dinner at my house. You'd never get past the first course at the Striped Bass."

"Leave off the sarcasm, kid. I can't help what I am."

"You could learn to be more playful, Dad," she responded. "You never take the time to have fun."

He gave her his standard reply. "You have it for me. How's your mother?"

Mary Ellen sighed, knowing she was the only link between her parents. They always asked after one another, which surprised her after all the fights and tears during the marriage over her father's lack of time for her mother. Or her. He was actually better with her now that she was an adult. Or maybe she had simply bullied her way into his appointment book until she stuck. "Mom's fine."

"Still in that social waste of time down there in Florida?"

That was the other half of the story: they always had

snippy comments to make about each other. Tonight her father used one of his favorites.

"Leave off the sarcasm, Poppy. She can't help what she is," Mary Ellen retorted. "Neither can you, remember? You're the one who likes to run corporations and banks to the exclusion of all else."

"Yeah." Her dad sipped his wine. "You're right. I know I'm a workaholic. Your mom knows she's a socialite. We knew it before we got married, but we could never compromise."

Mary Ellen wondered if her father still had feelings for her mother. And her mother for him. It seemed to her that if their love were dead, neither would ask how the other was. Maybe once or twice a year at Christmas and Easter or something, but not every time.

She looked closely at her father. He was good-looking still, with a barrel chest held in check from near daily treadmill workouts. Granted, he had female companionship from time to time, but he'd always seemed to be a rock unto himself. Mary Ellen realized he was lonely. He had thrown himself into his work for so long that he had nothing to take its place when it no longer satisfied him. Except giving grants.

"Why don't you retire and go back to school, Dad?" she suggested.

His mouth dropped open. "What the hell's that all about?"

She shrugged. "I don't know. You seem...wistful tonight. Obviously, you like education, with the foundation and all. Why not truly follow it and go back to school?"

"You've blown a gasket, girl."

"Probably," she agreed.

She served up dinner, the linguini in clam sauce forestalling further conversation for a time.

"Exquisite," her father told her after the first few bites. "I always thought you would have made a decent chef. It surprised me that you never opened a restaurant."

"Too much hard work." She grinned. "I have fun at my job. I've got the women's pro basketball team coming in to play the U.S. Olympic team in late spring. We'll draw about ten thousand, I think. That's conservative."

Her dad nodded. "You've latched on to the leading edge, like your old man. We're a lot alike. You just bull ahead like me when you want something."

She chuckled. "You flatter me."

"I checked up on Peter Holiday."

Mary Ellen's fork paused halfway to her mouth. She realized what she was doing and shoved the food into her mouth. The linguini tasted like ashes. She chewed and swallowed anyway. "Really? Why? What's the problem?"

"You shot him in the backside, that's the problem. I wanted to make sure he was healing right, so he wouldn't sue your backside off in return. Or mine. It happened at the house, after all."

If only her father knew how intimate Peter truly was with her derriere, he'd know a lawsuit was the last thing on Peter's mind. "It was an accident, Dad. Peter knows that."

"Maybe. But he could still nail us."

Mary Ellen bristled. "Peter's a good guy, Dad. Honest, hardworking and...honest. He plays fair with people."

Her father's eyes narrowed. "How the hell do you know all that about him?"

She had stepped onto dangerous ground, she decided. Now she had to back off of it. "I've met him a few times, remember? We've chatted in a friendly manner. He's nice. That's obvious."

"You were kissing him that day at the Striped Bass."

Her father had thrown her back on the dangerous turf. "I'll admit he's attractive in a bookish sort of way. But I remembered what you told me about innocents, Dad."

She was telling the truth...just not all of it.

"See that you do remember. Like I told you before, you'd kill a guy like that."

"Thanks a bunch," she muttered. Her own father thought she was a vamp or worse. "Your *high* opinion of me means so much."

"I do have a high opinion of you." Her father patted her hand, a rare gesture of affection. "I can see you like the guy, but you'd get bored with him fast. And he's not equipped to handle that. These scientists are smart as hell, yet know nothing about being human. They're all surface creatures, like little kids. You're a grown woman. You were engaged before, so I know you've...well, you know what I'm saying. Most of these guys are so wrapped up in their work, they're duds...in other places. And they're never home, like me. You'd hate that, like your mother, and want out, naturally, but he wouldn't understand. He'd actually be more hurt than you would. That's how you'd kill him. You'd break his heart."

Mary Ellen wished she could tell him he was stereotyping—boy, was he stereotyping!—but she clamped her lips shut. Nodding, she finally said, "I can see that, Dad."

"Good. Besides, any fooling around with him complicates his grant application. He's got a good project on emotional behavior imbalances. I wouldn't want to see that automatically taken out of contention because you meddled in something you shouldn't."

"Isn't that unfair?" Mary Ellen asked, feeling she had a legitimate opening. "It seems to me that who he's seeing shouldn't affect the grant application...I am speaking theoretically."

She was questioning totally on theory, in a detached manner. Absolutely.

"It better be theoretical." Her father paused. "In a perfect world, maybe. But this isn't a perfect world. The foundation's credibility would be marred. I've spent the past ten years ensuring that wouldn't happen. That's why I make the final decision myself on where the money goes. Candidates might be able to get to the pros on the committee that advises me, but they can't get to me."

His concern only confirmed that Peter was a serious contender. She might not agree with Peter's theory about love and chemical imbalances, but the "pros" clearly thought it had merit. An urge, as compelling as anything she'd experienced thus far, came over her to refute Peter's theory as dangerous. Yet that would betray Peter. She couldn't do that and live with herself afterward. Her heart and her head warred, leaving her confused and silent. Finally, her heart won.

"I'm sure everyone knows you can't be compromised, Dad. But you have nothing to worry about."

Just a daughter dead from love starvation long before he ever made his damned decision on the grant.

"THE FUNDING RUNS OUT in two months, Peter. Nothing can be done about it. Believe me, I've tried."

Peter stared at Jim Banner, his center's university sponsor. "You're kidding. You've got to be kidding."

"No. The federal government is cutting back on the budget, and frankly, research funding is in a bloodbath. We'll no longer get their money, and that shrinks our ability to fund projects like the Hartman study you're doing for us."

"That study is only half through its proper course," Peter argued. He had spent so long building the center's projects, he couldn't believe one actually wouldn't be completed. Worse, the reduction affected all the other projects at the center—including his emotional-behavior study. "You're throwing away five years of work, Jim. You know the government needs that information on current behavior trends, to project future criminal activity. How the hell else will they stop rising crime? Don't they realize the work already done was directly responsible for promoting antidrug programs to the younger children. You can't dump Hartman like this."

Hartman was the name of the repeat offender whose early life—both genetic and environmental factors— formed the basis for the original study. Now the Hartman project, one of the biggest the center had, was threatened. By stupidity in Washington.

"I'm sorry, Peter," Jim said. "We're doing all we can to get private sponsorship. But it won't be enough and we know it. There's a slim chance the budget won't get passed, so lobby your congressmen."

"I don't have time to lobby my congressmen!" Peter shouted, losing control. He took a deep breath and outwardly calmed down. His insides churned, however, the bile in his stomach rising in his throat.

"You'll have to make time." His sponsor rose and shrugged on his coat. "I'm sorry, Peter. We've all got to face economic reality."

Peter wanted to rail against the system that made commitments, then pulled the rug out without warning. After showing Jim out, he noticed people hovering around his office. They had been around research long enough to know the score.

These people depended on the center, he realized. They could go homeless if he had to close. Maybe that was too drastic a reaction. Then again, he had seen studies on the types of people who actually became homeless. Losing everything wasn't so farfetched. Even having these people not be able to work in their field of expertise would be a tragedy.

Mary Ellen flitted through his mind. He wanted to call her, just to share his bad news. He'd never had a need like that before—to reach out for comfort—and he couldn't explain his need now. Mary Ellen was Mary Ellen, and he wanted to hear her voice. He wanted to thank her, too. Her concern about jeopardizing his grant application might mean the difference between closing his research center's doors or not.

But his own personal need would have to wait. He had responsibilities that demanded his attention right now. He squared his shoulders and called everyone into the conference room, preferring to prepare them for what was coming rather than spring it on them in the form of pink slips.

They sat, stunned then angry.

"Isn't there anything we can do?" Matthew asked.

"Jim said to lobby Congress," Peter replied. "But I don't have time, with the other studies—"

"To hell with them!"

"They may go, too, if we don't save Hartman."

Everybody started speaking at once. Peter realized his colleagues wanted to fight for the Hartman study. They needed to and, truthfully, so did he.

"Okay!" he shouted. "Let's set a goal and determine a way to get there!"

Everyone began shuffling papers and writing furiously, huddling in work groups until the center had a plan of action, plus several alternatives to regarner funding. It was well after midnight when Peter got home, exhausted and pretty much brain-dead. He didn't bother with the answering machine or its blinking light. He collapsed in his bed and slept like a corpse.

Round two started the next morning. Peter juggled six chores at once, including a series of phone calls from other research facilities with their own similar bad news. Everyone must have been hit at the same time, he thought. He had it in his mind to call Mary Ellen the moment he had a break. Only he never had one. He felt as if he was swimming upstream and losing the battle.

He found himself agreeing to go to a hastily called coalition meeting in St. Louis. Half of him balked at the price of the same-day ticket. The other half won the argument on the theory that a group effort could net results better than one voice and that he'd better get his backside there to be a part of it.

Two days later, he was home again, better enlightened but not more hopeful. No one truly knew what to do. As he dropped his overnight bag by his desk, he noticed his voice-mail message light blinking furiously. He groaned. The last thing he needed was more calls.

Then he remembered he still had to make one of his own.

He dialed Mary Ellen's office number, hoping she would still be at work at five in the afternoon. To his relief, she answered on the first ring.

"Thank God!" he said, sitting in his office chair. "I was afraid I'd miss you."

"I thought I'd missed you," she replied. Her voice sounded wonderful. "I left a ton of messages at your home and office."

"Was that you?" he asked, delighted.

"Somehow, I'm not so thrilled as you that you haven't checked your messages."

"I didn't do it deliberately. I've been in St. Louis."

"St. Louis! What the heck were you doing in St. Louis?"

He told her about the study and the ensuing events.

"Peter!" she exclaimed, her voice all-sympathy, just as he needed. "Why didn't you call me right away? I would have come over—"

"No!" he blurted. His stomach churned. "Much as I want you to, you can't, Mary Ellen. I *have* to get the Magnussen Foundation grant now. My center won't survive if I don't. I never realized before how many people depend on me for their living until I had this wake-up call. I can't destroy this."

"You're a serious contender, Peter, if it helps to know that."

"How do *you* know that? Mary Ellen, you didn't—"

"Relax, relax. My father volunteered the information over dinner the other night. Mostly, he was concerned that you wouldn't sue me over the arrow."

"Why would I do that?" he asked, bewildered. "It was a complete accident."

"Right on cue with the innocence. Peter, what can I do for you? I know people and politicians. I could get a good lobbyist friend of mine to take on your cause, although he costs the earth—"

"Which I don't have."

"I was right about us not seeing each other, wasn't I?" she asked. "We can't even sneak in a coatroom soiree anymore."

Peter laughed bitterly. "No soirees, no matter how much I wish I could hold you right now. Believe me, I desperately need to hold you."

"Oh, Peter."

That little melting sound in her voice sent him over the edge. He loved being the cause of it. She always surprised him. She always made him feel as if he was the most important man in the world. Oddly, his brain chose that moment to wonder if she made any other man feel the same way. He hoped not.

"I wish I could have your help in this," he said, not too proud to admit the truth. "But maybe it's better under the circumstances if you're not involved. You could steer me in the direction of anybody you think could help me with funding, however. Any politician who might listen."

She gave him several names right off the top of her head. Even better, she gave him the names of their aides, who could get him past the normal roadblocks.

"And hold a press conference," she added.

"Whatever for?"

"The public wants crime reduced. Your study could cut into that effort greatly, and yet the government wants to eliminate it. That'll tick people off, because of the high crime numbers that are always coming out, which scare the heck out of them. Congress would think twice about cutting funding on a project like yours, if enough fuss is raised. Get out there and raise the fuss.''

Peter gulped. ''But a press conference...I have no clue how to do that.''

She told him exactly how. Why he had ever thought her flighty, he couldn't imagine. She reminded him of a general directing a battle—and knowing how to get an easy win.

''You're magnificent,'' he said at last.

''I'm better than that. Valentine's Day was your lucky day.''

''Absolutely.''

She sighed. He knew what she meant. She wanted to see him, but not as much as he wished he could see her.

He called her again that night, wanting to tell her about his progress. He knew he was torturing himself, but he couldn't break all contact with her. He needed to share what he could of himself with her. He believed love was caused by a chemical imbalance and was testing the antidote he'd come up with right now, on mice in the lab, yet a part of him was almost relieved that the funding crisis had hit. It was as if he didn't want to cure love, let alone the other emotions mankind had. Everything confused him so much right now, and he knew he would feel better if he could talk to Mary Ellen.

But the telephone rang and rang, going unanswered.

Disappointed, he hung up and went in to take a needed shower. He was pulling on clean briefs afterward when his doorbell rang.

His heart pounded. She wouldn't. He couldn't. He shouldn't even open the door.

He did. She had.

Mary Ellen stood on his doorstep. She wore a man's coveralls, a baseball cap...and a thick, dark, handlebar mustache.

"I've come to fix the plumbing," she said in a gruff voice, while grinning from ear-to-ear. Her blue eyes sparkled. She held up two small, square packages. "I even brought the safety equipment."

"Thank God!" He pulled her across the threshold and slammed the door shut against any prying eyes.

He kissed her. Her mustache tickled.

Chapter Seven

"Put the mustache on again."

Mary Ellen burst out laughing. She rolled on top of Peter's wonderfully naked length. "You're getting downright kinky, Peter."

"No, I'm not." He reached over to the nightstand and picked up the mustache. "Put it on again."

"Freud would have a lot to say about this."

"Screw Freud."

"He'd probably say that first." She took the mustache and pressed it under her nose. "Happy?"

He grinned and kissed her. The edges of the mustache hairs tickled her upper lip and cheek, adding an odd erotic sensation to the ones already flowing rampantly inside her. His hands played up and down her spine, sending more delicious shivers throughout her body.

When he eased his mouth away, he said, "Now I'm happy."

She peeled off the mustache. "I know I shouldn't have come here tonight, but you sounded like you needed a friend."

"And a lover," he admitted. "I know I said all those things about being circumspect. I know this could be the most disastrous thing if your father finds out. But I needed to see you, to hold you like this.''

She had needed more than that. When he hadn't returned her calls, she had panicked, thinking he didn't want to see her anymore. She hadn't known what she had done to offend or disgust him. His lack of response had sent a shaft of pain through her, intense and devastating.

Even after finding out about the problems he was facing, she had still needed to assure herself that he wanted her. Granted, his chemical-imbalance theory was a big problem with her. But major alarm bells had gone off in her head when he'd immersed himself in his work. She knew he was facing a crisis. She wanted to help him. But she had come here tonight to reassure herself that he wasn't revealing a workaholic side of himself. Days of unanswered calls certainly hadn't reassured her. Her father had even suggested it the night they'd had dinner. An inner voice had screamed in horror about the risk she took while she drove over to Peter's house. But she could no more stop herself than she could stop the wind.

She kissed his bare chest. ''I'm glad you wanted me to come tonight.''

He whispered something earthy in her ear. Very earthy. She giggled.

''You've been a tremendous help already,'' he said. ''I did get into Congressman Walker's inner sanctum.''

''You talked to Jerry?'' Jerry was Walker's top aide and an old friend of Mary Ellen's.

''Yes. Nice lady. She was very excited and thought she could stir up the law-enforcement committee about the impact of the cuts. Walker's chairman of that.''

Peter kissed her again.

Later, after some even more ardent and more poignant lovemaking, Mary Ellen lay in Peter's embrace, exhausted yet fighting sleep. She had to leave soon, while still under the cover of darkness. She ran her fingers through the soft hair on his chest, lifting the strands and marveling at the way they felt against her skin.

"My skin seems so smooth against yours," she said.

"It's smoother."

"Don't get all logical on me again."

"But you are smoother, like silk. Or is it satin?" He caressed her arm and shoulder, his hand strong and warm, yet sending chills along her nerves. "I can't decide which description fits, but your skin...God, but I love touching it, Mary Ellen."

"I love touching you." She did, especially now. "Peter, everything we try to do to control our...need for each other backfires. It's as if the more we know we shouldn't, the more forbidden our being together becomes, and the more we can't help it."

"Our timing is bad. Two, three months from now and there would be no ban on whatever we wanted to do, whenever and wherever we wanted to do it. Well, maybe just general laws on indecency. But that's all."

She raised her head. "Maybe you're right. Maybe if we didn't have all these reasons to keep apart, we wouldn't want each other at all."

"I didn't say that."

"Good." Relief washed through her. She needed to know something more was involved here besides forbidden lust. She ought to ask where this relationship was going, but she wasn't ready to face an answer yet. Besides, she needed time to bring him around to her way of thinking about love and commitment. Walking away now would be giving in to her fear of failure. She had to stay until she made it a success.

"Mary Ellen…"

"Mmm?"

"We've really got to be careful."

"I know. My father made that clear."

"No more wigs and mustaches."

"I didn't wear a wig."

"No more mustaches."

She smiled against his skin. "Are you sure you want that? You seem to have a thing about them."

"Okay, just the mustache." He rubbed her arm. "Why should I deny myself?"

"Why should *we?* Because if you're going to be kinky, I'll be kinky, too."

"Right."

"This isn't fair," she said, thinking of the way they had to control themselves in public. In private they were a complete failure at control. But why couldn't they be like the rest of the world and just face everything, letting the chips fall where they may?

She already knew the answer to the question: because of the center and the people who worked there. Even if there were no others dependent on the grant, she would never forgive herself if he lost it because of his involvement with her. She wanted to convince Peter he was on the wrong track entirely with his current study and have him voluntarily give it up.

"Life never promised to be fair," Peter said. "We just have to work with what we're given."

"Out of the mouths of babes."

After she left him in the small hours of the morning, she felt buoyed somehow. Their separations were torture, but she thought they had now found a way around them. Peter had said they would have to be very careful, but he hadn't said they would no longer see each other. He hadn't said they would be reduced to only phone contact again because of the crisis. That was important. He wasn't a workaholic. She had only responded to a primal fear.

Best of all, the more physical contact they had, the closer they would grow. The closer they grew, the more Peter would see that love could be good, something to be trusted, not a time bomb waiting to go off, with disastrous results. Now, instead of being reduced to using the telephone, they would sneak around.

She got it. She was logical.

Her only worry, besides the obvious one, was that their feelings for each other stemmed from the forbidden nature of their relationship more than anything else. She knew the word *no* was like a red flag being waved in front of her. Never liking to be told she couldn't do something, she responded instantly in the opposite direction.

To receive a definitive answer on whether they were experiencing forbidden lust, she would have to let this run to its natural end. However their relationship played out, she would accept it. Peter was different from any man she had met before—honest and innocent, gentle and strong, stubborn and forgiving.

She pushed aside the feeling that she would never be ready for a natural ending with him, no matter how much she prepared herself for it.

Instead, she planned their next "forbidden" meeting.

"I CAN'T," Peter said, not able to stifle a chuckle of amusement.

"Please. It's dinner at one of the worst diners in the city," Mary Ellen wheedled over the telephone. "No one will ever see us together."

Good thing she was on the phone. He'd never resist her in person. But he had to today. He was swamped with work. "I've got to do a presentation tomorrow in Washington for the law-enforcement committee. I'll be working all night."

"You've got to eat. I could deliver it. And I promise I'll *deliver*."

"Oh, God," Peter moaned, envisioning himself supping on her creamy flesh. Kissing every freckle… "Mary Ellen, don't even think it. I've got a ton of people here tonight who *don't* need impulsive-behavior lessons. I'm only a man, after all."

"Hell."

"That's where I'm at right now."

"Tomorrow night then, after you get back from Washington."

"Working."

"Friday."

"Working."

"Weekend."

"Working."

"When *aren't* you working?"

"Nineteen ninety-nine?"

"You sound a little too happy for someone who's working."

In some ways, he did feel invigorated. Directing everyone toward a common cause, fighting for his beliefs, his life's work and the others' livelihoods had brought a level of excitement and enthusiasm that surprised him. Yet none of that was close to what he felt about Mary Ellen.

Why? Why her? Was it the fact that she was forbidden which made her so attractive to him? He still had no answer, only more need to explore all the facets of Mary Ellen. But he couldn't tempt himself right now. He had risked much the other night. He didn't hold a single regret, but he couldn't take a chance and see her again so soon. The more they saw of each other, the more likely they would blunder into someone who could give them away. A lot of Jeremys were out there.

"I'm not happy," he said. "I'm overwhelmed."

"You can't find a moment for us tonight?"

"If I could, I would, but there just aren't any. Maybe it's good that I'm so busy, Mary Ellen. We won't be tempted to see each other. Not with the center in trouble like it is and needing your father's foundation grant now."

Silence reigned on the other end of the telephone.

"Mary Ellen? Please. Bear with me a little longer."

He heard a sigh. "All right, Peter. I do know you have a lot of problems facing you and not much time to solve them."

Relieved, he said, "Thank you."

"Promise me, though, that if you ever want to break it off, you'll flat out tell me."

He frowned. "Why would you say that?"

"I just want us to be straight with each other."

"I've always been straight with you."

"I feel the same way. I would tell you up front if I wanted to break it off."

He swallowed. "Do you? Want to break it off?"

"No." The answer came quickly.

"Me, neither." He thought of the other night and tried a joke. "Let's keep being straight with each other. Very straight."

"I hope so."

Her voice sounded tired—and unamused. He sensed something else in her tone, too. It sent a prickle of warning across his senses. He wished he had more experience with women to interpret the wary sensation. Fortunately, he knew someone who did.

He called his cousin Michael. Michael always spoke of avoiding marriage, yet he always had a woman on his arm. Michael understood women a whole lot more than Peter knew he ever would. After asking after Michael's newspaper columns, he got down to business. "I'm seeing a woman, Michael."

"There's a miracle."

"Thanks," Peter muttered. Michael's wit was too dry sometimes.

"I'm teasing you. You're such a great target, always so serious."

"I'm a better target than you think," Peter said, reminded of his wounded rear end. Valentine's Day would never be the same again. "This woman I'm seeing is exciting, different, but there are complications...obstacles, let's say, that tell me I shouldn't be seeing her at all. I don't want to stop, but now she's distant, kind of funny and she talked about breaking up—"

"Did she ask you if you wanted to break up with her?" Michael asked.

Peter's jaw dropped, amazed that his cousin had guessed right. "Yes."

"That just means she's unsure of you. Most women who do that want reassurance from the man. That means you're in the driver's seat with this relationship. Way to go, Peter."

"But I don't know how I did that," Peter admitted, feeling a little better.

"Doesn't matter, my friend. Just enjoy it."

"Are you sure?" he asked, wanting to be certain. He couldn't imagine Mary Ellen putting him in the driver's seat. She'd be more likely to fight him for the wheel, if not win it outright.

"As sure as every woman who's ever asked me that question. But be careful. When women ask this, they usually want more than you're currently giving to the relationship."

"Oh." Peter smiled. "That explains it completely. My work's interfering with our being able to see each other." He told his cousin about the funding crisis. "That's probably why she's been so unsure."

"A bouquet of flowers will fix it...if you want it fixed. It all depends on how far you want the relationship to go. My personal advice is don't send the flowers. Not being able to see a woman because of too much work gives you a graceful out with her. For one thing, what can she complain of without looking selfish? And second, she'll break it off with you first— which avoids a lot of screaming and crying, because she's less likely to want to kill you when she's the dumper rather than the dumpee. I *always* allow the woman to dump me."

Before Peter could reply, Matthew rushed through his office door. "The computer just dumped the files! We've lost the figures for the first year's study!"

Peter cursed at being an unexpected dumpee. He needed those numbers for the congressional presentation tomorrow. Into the telephone, he said, "I have to go."

He hung up on his cousin and raced out of his office,

Matthew following. Michael's words were forgotten in the disaster.

In a repeat of the initial crisis over the center's funding, several days went by before Peter was able to call Mary Ellen. He deliberately waited until the night, so they could have one of "their calls."

"I miss you," he said, as soon as she answered the telephone.

"Who is this?"

He gaped, astonished. "Peter! Who the hell did you think it was?"

"Oh. How's the crisis going?"

"Like a crisis, but I didn't call to talk about that."

"Well, what do you want? It's late."

Something was wrong here. Very wrong. Belatedly, he remembered his cousin's advice about sending flowers to fix it—if he wanted it fixed. He did, but he'd have to fix it without flowers now. "You sound annoyed with me. Mary Ellen, I can't help my problems with the center. I just have to deal with them. Please try to understand."

"I do." Her voice softened, easing his anxiety. "I do understand too well."

That sounded strange. He didn't know very much about women, but this didn't sound like her at all. She was normally upbeat and teasing. It couldn't be just the hours he had had to put in. She had encouraged him to find solutions, had even sent him in the proper direction to achieve them. So why would she be distant now? Maybe she just needed more verbal reassurance...and fun.

He tried again. "I'm lying here naked—"

"Peter, I have an early meeting in the morning. Could we talk later?"

"Sure." What the hell else could he say?

Angry and hurt, he hung up the telephone. Somehow, somewhere, something was terribly wrong with Mary Ellen. He thought about Michael's suggestion of leaving things be for a "graceful" out. Peter knew in his heart he didn't want a graceful out. He wanted her.

He had to fix it. But how?

MARY ELLEN PUSHED A WISP of hair away from her face and tried to concentrate on her novel. The trials and tribulations of a woman on the brink of insanity swam before her unfocused eyes. Besides, the plot hit too damn close to home for her.

She hadn't heard from Peter in three days, not after that last telephone call. Obviously, she had put him off too well...but he had it coming. One call in over a week? *Working.* On some logical level, she knew he had to. On another, she knew they shouldn't be seeing each other right now because of her father and the grant. On yet another, she felt time was running out to change Peter's mind about eliminating romantic love.

But on the other hand, she found his ease in putting her off far too reminiscent of her father's attitude with her mother. *I'm working this hard for you. I thought you understood my job. People depend on me. I have to work like this. You know it has to be this way.*

She had heard all the excuses. None, she knew, would solve her loneliness. She didn't want to become her mother, clinging and bitter. Neither did she want a man who would shunt her aside without a backward glance. She needed to have her man around. She was discovering she didn't handle absence well, no matter how noble the reason.

This had to work with Peter. Somewhere, in her

heart of hearts, she wanted him to realize his theory about chemical imbalances was flawed. She wanted him to know that instead of providing a better quality of life, taking away romantic love would turn humanity into robots. But she didn't want it to be an issue of contention between them.

Only having Peter working at her father's pace and liking it—for he clearly did, despite the terrible pressures on him—had shaken her to the core. She had never expected this, never seen it coming in all the problems that they faced. Like the arrow she'd shot on Valentine's Day, his had reached an unexpected mark.

And it hurt. Really hurt.

Her doorbell rang. Her head shot up. Her heart pounded. Hope gripped her soul.

Get real, she thought. The last person it would be was Peter. Not straight-arrow Peter. More than likely it was Girl Scouts selling cookies at eleven at night.

She opened the door.

Peter stood there in coveralls, a black wig and a full, white beard. His grin peeked through. He held out a piece of evergreen. "I would have brought a flower but it's too early in the season to steal one from your garden. So, lady, have any plumbing that needs fixing? What does that mean, anyway?"

"Peter." She sucked in her breath, then reached out and dragged him inside. Shutting the door, she said, "You never should have come here. What if someone saw you?"

"They'd probably think I'm a nut."

"And I'm one for letting you in."

He pulled her to him before she could stop him. "Kiss me, woman."

Mary Ellen braced her hands between them. Tilting

her head away from his lowering mouth, she said, "Not with that thing on."

He stopped, looking so hurt that any pretense of distance melted away. She pulled the beard down, past his chin, and kissed him. "That's better." Then she let the fake beard snap back into place.

"Ouch!" He rubbed his lip. "That hurt."

"It could have been an arrow."

"True."

He kissed her again. This time they both got a mouthful of beard. Peter yanked it off and tried again. His mouth settled firmly on hers, his tongue instantly seeking hers out.

Mary Ellen gave herself up to the kiss. She knew she shouldn't, but that didn't matter. She wanted Peter. And he had come to her. Come to her! Risking everything to be with her showed an underlying emotional need. The promise was actually coming to fruition. She hoped. At least it was a start in the right direction. Wrapping her arms tightly around his neck, she kissed him back fully. Sensations shot through her, need foremost among them.

She pushed the silly wig off his head and ran her fingers through his hair. It brushed his collar. He needed a trim, she thought. Reminded of the cause, his heavy workload, she immediately pushed the notion aside. He was here now—and real. What more could she want?

More of him.

When the kiss finally ended, she took his hand and led him to the stairs.

"Are we going where I hope we are?" he asked.

She glanced back and grinned. "I have some etchings to show you. Naked women with mustaches."

"Oh, boy."

He began to run up the steps, passing her in his haste. She ran faster, turning it into a game. Laughing, she turned into her bedroom while he flew past the door, not familiar with her home. Skidding to a halt, he backtracked and grabbed her up, dumping her on the bed.

"I win," she said.

"Only because you knew where the bedroom was."

"A technicality."

"Shut up."

He kissed her. The desire roared back tenfold. Their mouths twisted and turned as if they needed to devour each other. Mary Ellen's breath came in gasps. She pressed herself against him. His body was already ready, like her own. She didn't want to wait. She couldn't.

She unsnapped the first buttons of the overalls. Peter's fingers went to her shirt. They divested each other of their clothes, kissing skin as it was revealed.

"You are so beautiful," she murmured, running her palms along his chest. She trailed her hands down his stomach, watching his muscles contract in reaction.

"Mary Ellen..." Peter whispered, his voice ragged.

"Vulnerable..." she continued, touching him intimately. "You're just out there, for the world to see every response. You can't hide it. You can't fake it."

"And women are hidden, mysterious," he said, stroking her breast, her stomach. He pressed his hand to her woman's flesh. "You allow me in, and when you do, you willingly make yourself more vulnerable than a man. I won't ever hurt you. I promise."

He would hurt her, she thought. He just wouldn't realize he did so. He was innocent in so many ways.

She smiled, not answering. Instead, she pulled his head down to her breasts.

He kissed and nipped and sucked until she was a writhing mass of need under his ministrations. She could smell the woody scent of his shampoo, mixed with the unique scent of him. She could also smell the heat of sex. Her desire flared to even more impossible heights. What was it about this man, who surprised her and pleased her in ways she'd never experienced before?

She could stand it no more. She pushed him on his back and kissed her way down his body. His flesh tasted hot and faintly salty. She nipped at his lower belly, teasingly avoiding anything more intimate.

Peter moved restlessly. His hands knotted in her hair. He moaned, yet didn't urge her forward. Feeling incredibly female and powerful, Mary Ellen covered him with her mouth. He whispered things. She didn't hear them clearly, concentrating only on torturing him as deliciously as he had tortured her.

Her body tingled. Her flesh burned for him. Her blood flowed thickly in her veins. Her own need overwhelmed her, but she fought for control. She wanted Peter as hungry as he made her. She wanted him to feel like he would never get enough of her. She wanted him to put her above all other things in his life.

She rose up and reached into her nightstand drawer. A moment later, the exercise in birth control turned into another form of sensual torture for him. She pushed him down, when he would have turned her on her back. Slowly, almost leisurely, she took the full length of him inside her.

"You're killing me," she whispered, feeling as if

she would shatter emotionally and physically from their being together.

He caressed her breasts. "You've made me a dead man ten times over."

She smiled and rose up, then thrust down, loving the feel of him within her hot, moist flesh. He met her in primitive rhythms of ageless mating. Mary Ellen arched her back, trying to take him impossibly deeper inside herself. Peter sat up and, wrapping his arms around about her, buried his face in her breasts. She clung to him, their passions riding higher and harder until the heat in her blood burst and throbbed in a thousand different directions. She cried out, pressing her face against Peter's hair, giving herself up to the devastating waves washing over her, inside of her.

Peter stiffened and groaned. She could feel his pulsing satisfaction within the most intimate part of her body.

She loved him.

Mary Ellen gasped at the realization. All the closeness, all the physical intimacy, spun and spun within her. She wanted to cry with pain and laugh with joy at the same time.

Pain won out.

"Mary Ellen," Peter said, taking her back down with him to the soft mattress.

He nestled her on top of him. She held him, still inside herself, and listened to his calming heartbeat. Her whole body felt distant and numb, as if she were outside her physical being looking down on them together.

He laughed—happily, innocently. "It keeps getting better and better."

She could say nothing, even though he was right.

Her heart squeezed tightly in her chest. She didn't believe her emotions were genuine. They couldn't be. What she really felt for him was affection and caring. She had the best sex she'd ever experienced in her life with him. But none of that meant love. It was the moment she responded to, that was all. The sex had overwhelmed her brain and she'd simply reacted the way a woman sometimes did after sex, just mistaking her feelings. "Peter."

"That's me."

She smiled and traced his face with shaking fingers. She kissed his hair. She said nothing. He raised his head, his gaze questioning.

"Oh, boy, does it get better and better," she said. She meant it, God help her.

But she wasn't in love. Definitely wasn't in love.

"THIS IS ANOTHER FINE MESS we've gotten ourselves into," Peter said, grinning at Mary Ellen while he dressed.

"Oh, no. You're not blaming this on me, my friend." She stretched against the flowered coverlet, her creamy body naked and extremely tempting. Peter wanted nothing more than to be tempted forever with her. But he knew the consequences would be severe. He risked so much already, but he hadn't been able to stay away.

"I can't resist you." He kissed her breasts, curling his tongue around her nipple.

Her eyes closed languidly. "That's better."

He straightened. "I don't know when I'll see you again."

She opened her eyes. "What do you mean?"

"I'll be tied up with the crisis," he replied. "I

shouldn't have even come tonight, because it's backed up a lot of work. And we do have that slight problem with your father and the grant.''

"We've found ways to see each other so far.''

"I know." He could go over all they should be doing—but who the hell was he kidding? They hadn't managed to stay away from each other yet. Control seemed to be a lost cause between them. "But we can't see each other too often. And we'll have to be extremely careful when we do.''

"Do you find all this sneaking around as sexy as I do?''

"More." He leaned over and kissed her stomach. He kissed her lower. "That's half the problem.''

"Do you think we're having a bad case of impossible opposites combined with forbidden lust? That it's just the danger and excitement that's attracted us? Are we recapturing our youth?''

He chuckled. "We're not that old." Running his fingers down her taut stomach, he added, "Definitely not that old.''

He kissed her. Echoes of the earlier passion mixed with the first stirrings of renewed need. She was naked and seductive in his arms. "God, Mary Ellen. Is the wanting always like this?''

She smoothed her hand down his cheek. "No. This is special.''

He smiled. He didn't understand this reaction he had about her, but it was way beyond chemical imbalances. At least, he knew now that it was extraordinary.

"I should go.''

She clung to him. "No. Please. Stay the night, Peter.''

"I want to." He pressed his face in her sweet-smelling hair. The floral scent invaded his senses, urging him to fling caution to the wind once again. He drew in a deep breath...and nearly lost his control. Firmly, he set her aside. "I can't stay. Don't tempt me."

She giggled. "You make me sound like Lola the Vamp and you're Peter the Preacher."

"That can be our next disguise."

He left her with a devastating kiss. On his way out, he picked up the discarded wig, chuckling that his deliberately silly masquerade had achieved the desired results. Very desired results. It had taken him days to clear some time for her, and by then he'd forgotten to get the flowers. Good thing he hadn't needed them.

Outside, in the silence of the late night, he whistled happily. Whatever had disturbed her before had vanished with their lovemaking. He could tell by the way she had clung to him and asked him to stay. Whatever was between them was safe and secure again. His father said friendship was the better binding agent between man and woman. Peter had friendship with Mary Ellen, and better still, fireworks in the intimacy.

A blinding flash of a revelation exploded inside him. That was it! He had what his father preached, and what he himself was trying to achieve through eliminating love. *Intimate friendship*. What more could a man ask for?

If only he could stay with Mary Ellen tonight, he thought, his whistling fading. He nearly turned around and went back inside. He couldn't, though, and he knew it. No sense tempting himself beyond redemption.

He began whistling again.

All was right with his world.

Chapter Eight

Mary Ellen felt like a tick about to pop.

Okay, so that overstated the case, she thought, while sitting through another interminable meeting of the sports-center staff. But something was happening behind the scenes. She could see the drawn face of the Sixers' current owner. The pro basketball team had done poorly for years now, and every move the owner made had seemed doomed, setting the team further back rather than propelling it forward. The pro-hockey-team owner, Ed Reisman, normally had a stoic expression despite his team's yearly successes. Today, he actually gave a little, smug smile.

Odd that both men were here, she thought, half listening to the arena manager. She worked for the hockey owner, in a way. His corporation also owned the sports center, but his decisions rarely affected her.

No, Peter was to blame for her restlessness. Things had not improved between them since their night together. She'd thought she might see more of him after his successful appearance in front of the congressional committee. The media had played the session up. People had called their representatives and complained about the cuts. It looked as if that wouldn't happen now.

She'd been patient, she admitted. She'd been willing to be circumspect. She had only wanted to see him, to wipe away the growing doubts within her about a future with this man. He couldn't be like her father. He couldn't.

But he was still "swamped."

"Get a damn alligator," she muttered, disgusted.

"Did you hear that?" her seat neighbor asked.

Mary Ellen glanced up. She realized the room was buzzing with excited voices. The arena manager was waving his arms for silence, but people weren't paying the least attention to him. "No, I missed it. What is it?"

"They're selling, the both of them. They're selling the teams and Reisman's selling the building to Keycast, the cable network. He'll still own a majority part of the hockey team, but he'll be a managing partner of the basketball team, too."

Mary Ellen gaped. "Are you kidding?"

"No. Listen."

She did. Shocked at the sudden change in her livelihood, she wanted to scrub her ears. They had to be clogged or damaged or something. This was so sudden. She had heard a rumor or two of something coming down, but she'd never expected anything like this. She wondered immediately about the security of her own job and staff.

It occurred to her that she was now in the same boat with Peter. She called him as soon as she reached her office.

"That's nice," he said, after she told him her news.

Anger rose inside her, like a pressure cooker on high.

"It's *not* nice, Peter. New owners clean house. I don't know if I'll have a job with the change in the center's management."

"But they would be crazy to fire you. You told me yourself you booked sixty dates. That's two full months! I don't know a thing about sports, but I can figure out that's good."

"They might not think it's good enough." She wanted to see him. She wouldn't ask. "How is your own 'crisis'?"

She'd only ask a little.

"Slightly better, but now we're behind in our other work."

"What else is new?" she muttered.

"I didn't catch what you said."

"Nothing. Trust me."

"You sound annoyed."

"Yes, I'm annoyed. And scared. I understood your crisis and was right there for you. Now I'm having one of my own. Men are clueless."

Peter cleared his throat. "Dumb, too… Okay, well, fight it, Mary Ellen. I know! Get your father to buy the building instead."

"No one is going to sell just days after they've bought. Even if they would, my father doesn't have the hundreds of millions needed." She paused, her stomach churning. Peter's words seemed flippant and they annoyed her. She usually coped well with change, but this had come from nowhere. How the top people had kept the sale hidden this long amazed her.

"Show them how important you are," Peter said. "How indispensable your division is to the building. Make them think they would be making a big mistake if they got rid of you."

She sucked in her breath. "You're right."

"Naturally. It's only logical."

"You're really living on that, aren't you?"

"Why not? It's only logical."

She laughed, suddenly wanting to kiss him for his logic. He made her feel better than she had a moment ago. "You're incorrigible, too, but that's beside the point. Thank you, Peter. You catch on to sympathy real fast. My moment of angst is over."

"Now you'll be as busy as me, that's for sure."

The words stunned her as effectively as a slap in the face. "That makes you really happy, doesn't it?"

"Mary Ellen, we have to take care of our work. People depend on us for their livings. We have to do what it takes to keep them and us secure. It's logical."

"Logic only goes so far." She hated logic suddenly. "You think it's okay to sacrifice ourselves on the altar of work? I don't."

"I'm not suggesting we sacrifice anything—"

"Yes, you are," she interrupted, her voice rising with her anger. "You think all this is perfectly fine, don't you?"

"We *have* to work. You're being unreasonable, Mary Ellen."

"No, I'm not. I still want to find time for you in all this, but you like work too much, Peter. I see that now."

"It's my life. I'm not ashamed of it. You've spent all this time with your father. Surely you've seen how research is more than a job."

"Nothing should be more important than the people you care about," she said. *"Nothing."*

"We're fighting over a temporary situation, Mary Ellen."

"That's what I'm afraid of, Peter—that it's not temporary," she said, knowing she had enough to do to try and change his mind about eliminating love. What if she couldn't? What if he turned out to be a real absentminded professor who simply forgot her needs?

She hung up the telephone a few moments later, feeling shaken, not stirred. Hardly stirred. Everything had gone wrong today.

People knocked on her office door, momentarily distracting her. After they came in, with tons of questions about the sale, she decided to let them continue to distract her. Peter was right in one respect. These people depended on her, and she should fight for them, if nothing else. She *would* show the new management that her division was indispensable…that she was indispensable and they would be idiots to get rid of her. And if they were idiots, then she'd wrap up one helluva résumé that managers of another arena couldn't resist.

When she finally left the building, after ten that night, she walked slowly to her car. In the parking lot, she noticed a tall figure waiting by her vehicle. Her heart stopped with fear, the hair on her neck rising for an instant. Then her heart stopped beating for another reason altogether. The person was Peter.

Gathering her control, she walked casually toward him. He unfolded his arms and straightened from her rear fender.

"I've been waiting for an hour. I didn't think you'd ever come out," he said.

The night held a leftover chill of winter that only added to the awkwardness between them. "Why didn't you come inside?"

He shrugged. "Didn't seem like a good idea, since you had a crisis to cope with. I also kept thinking you'd come out at any moment, so I didn't want to go home and miss you.''

"What happened to your own crisis?" Damn, she thought, horrified. She sounded just like her mother.

"I thought it could wait, because I figured you needed a hug." He looked away and back. "Maybe I was wrong."

She was about to apologize when she heard voices behind them. She turned and saw a small group of men coming through the parking lot. Under the halogen lights, she recognized the hockey owner, the arena manager and an old friend.

"Excuse me," she said to Peter. "Jack! Jack Crowley, is that you?"

The group stopped. One man left the others and came toward her. She went to meet him. He gave her a hug and a buss on the cheek.

"Mary Ellen, you sweet thing! How are you?"

"Fine." When she had first met Jack Crowley, he had been the trainer for the basketball team. He had parleyed his physical-therapy background into a chain of successful fitness centers before selling them last year for over a hundred-million dollars. She gazed at the loden green Armani suit, the red wool beret with its black leather piping, the fashionable teacup glasses, the shoulder-length ponytail and goatee. He looked about as far from the Horatio Alger story as the moon was to earth. "My, my, Jack. We are looking ultrahip these days. The ladies must be falling all over themselves. How's Meredith?"

"Happier being divorce number two, babe," he said, grinning wryly.

She shook her head. "For shame. What are you do-

ing here, anyway? You looking to take your job
back?''

His grin widened. "I've got a new one. Can you
keep a secret?'' He didn't wait for a reply. "Doesn't
matter. The press conference is in two days, so the
leaks are starting anyway. Mary Ellen, you are looking
at Keycast's new president of the basketball team and
a minority team owner besides. This deal is huge,
honey.''

She gaped at him. "Really?''

"That's what I said. Mind you, Harvey's still got to
sign the papers, which could be iffy.'' Harvey was the
basketball-team owner. "He loves the team and he really doesn't want to sell, although he knows it's best.
I've been after him for months about selling me a minority share of the team, but he insisted on an all-or-
nothing deal.'' Jack looked at her over the top of his
glasses. "I knew the Keycast people wanted to start a
sports channel and were looking for further invest-
ments. I went to them and put together a deal the
hockey guys liked and Harvey couldn't refuse. It took
less money from me to boot.''

Mary Ellen laughed, delighted for him. "You come
up smelling like roses every time, Jack Crowley.''

"Beats wrapping ankles and feet, which do smell
big-time after a game. Hey, you've been doing great
here. The Keycast people were really happy with your
numbers.''

"I hope that means I still have a job.''

"Why the hell wouldn't you? Some will be gone,
which I hate to see. They were people I worked with
when I was here. I wish they hadn't let the ride take
them along, rather than being behind the wheel like
they should have been. But you're definitely not one

of them." He suddenly swung her around in a circle. "Wooee, girl! We are gonna have some fun!"

Her job was safe and secure. Relieved, Mary Ellen hugged him back. She realized she had left Peter standing by her car. It didn't matter, she thought happily, while disentangling herself from Jack's exuberance.

She rushed over to tell Peter the great news.

PETER WATCHED MARY ELLEN hug the man, this Jack Crowley. If he'd got the name right.

Who cared about the name, he thought, doing a slow burn. He had come to give her a hug and she'd received it from someone else. She looked too damn…joyous with the clown. And what was with that hat?

Peter had come here thinking she needed him. He had waited outside in the cold for her. And for what? His mind urged him to go, to leave her with this man she flaunted in front of him. Yet he stayed, fuming as he did.

She finally deigned to return to him. "The sports gods are looking down on me. That was Jack Crowley."

"So I heard," he said, wishing he didn't sound so clipped.

"Yes, he's…" She grabbed his arm and looked around. "We can't talk here, Peter, where people could hear us. There's a hoagie shop on Delaware Avenue. Follow me there."

She gave him no time to agree or refuse, hopping in her car no sooner than the words were out. He got into his car more slowly and did follow her, cursing himself the entire time.

The sandwich shop was small, with only a few tables. The take-out line was long, however. The employees greeted Mary Ellen familiarly. Peter felt like a third wheel. Or was it fifth? Whatever, he was out of his element.

Their secret was still safe. This place would hardly be swarming with people who knew her father. Personally, Peter didn't much care who saw them right now. He had more important things to deal with.

"So, who is this Jack Crowley?" he asked, when they were seated.

"The Easter Bunny, Saint Patrick and Santa Claus all rolled into one," she said. She gripped his hand, her fingers tight around his. "Peter, this can't go any further, but Jack is one of the new partners in the Keycast deal. In fact, he's a major mover and shaker behind it!"

"He sounds like an earthquake."

She giggled. "Hurricane is more like it. Jack's always been an upbeat person whose personality just sweeps over you."

Peter bet he was. He hadn't missed the way the man had pressed Mary Ellen to him. His hand had been mere inches from her backside. If any man was touching her on the derriere, it should be he, Peter Holiday. After all, she hadn't shot him in the tush for nothing. He had a proprietary claim on that part of the anatomy, hers and his.

He realized she was chattering on about Jack Crowley. He wanted to shut her up with a kiss—with more— but he doubted the hoagie people would be thrilled. Better to let her talk, to find out exactly what her relationship was, past, present and future, with Jack Crowley.

But by the time she finished her litany, Peter's stomach churned. Crowley had gone from humble beginnings to multimillionaire in ten short years. Worse, he was some kind of do-gooder. At least that was what Peter gathered from her stories of Crowley taking depressed people and sticking with them until they regained a positive outlook on life again.

"And he's a motorcycle freak," she added for good measure.

Peter's heart sank. Mary Ellen made Crowley sound like some bad-boy wonder. Was there nothing the man couldn't do? She also sounded like a one-woman admiration society for Jack. That *really* bothered Peter. All he had going for himself was an arrow in the rear end on Valentine's Day.

"You sound like you know him well."

"I did, but I haven't seen him more than once or twice in the past few years."

"Then he's an old *friend.*"

"Sure."

"You seem so easy with him." He decided to ask a burning question. Or rather, the question burning him. "Did you date him?"

She laughed. "Jack tried to date everybody back then."

"Oh. So he's bisexual."

She burst into laughter, turning heads around them. "God, no! Why ever would you think that?"

"You said he dated *everyone.*"

"I meant women."

"I see."

She smiled. "He told me the Keycast people were happy with my performance. My division's secure."

"That's good, Mary Ellen." Peter smiled back, happy for her. He just wished he were truly happy at the moment. Why would her old "friendship" with

Jack Crowley bother him so much? Because that's what he had with her now—an intimate friendship that had the promise of a lifetime in it. He didn't want to know she felt that way about anyone else. "Is Jack married?"

Might as well ask that second burning question.

"Not anymore." She giggled. She actually giggled. "He's a hopeless romantic. Unfortunately, he can't stick with one woman much past the initial romance."

Peter perked up. This was definitely promising. "He sounds like a candidate for my research."

"You leave Jack just the way he is," she said, sobering. "It's up to him to change. Not you to change him with some antidote."

Clearly, she liked Crowley as a ladies' man. That didn't sound so promising, after all. She was too animated talking about Jack Crowley as it was.

Peter pushed the thought away. A scientist gathered as much information as he could before he ever projected any conclusion. He'd better keep that in mind. "How closely will you be working with him?"

"Oh, not too closely, I would guess. He'll be heavily involved with the basketball team." Her eyes gleamed. "Do you have any idea how big this deal is?"

"Not a clue," Peter admitted cheerfully, feeling better that she would rarely see Jack Crowley.

"It's huge," she replied. "If it goes through. The basketball owner still has to sign the contracts. It could blow up. Pray it doesn't."

"Why?" Peter asked, puzzled. "You'll just be back to the status quo."

She shook her head. "Not now. Even if this deal doesn't go through for some reason, the world knows the teams and building were for sale. More offers will come in, and one will stick. I know where I stand with this one, but I can't say that for the next. Besides, Jack is such a positive force with anything he touches that I sense big things with this deal—''

''But you said earlier that no one will buy right after a sale,'' he interrupted, totally confused.

''I said the new buyer wouldn't sell a few days after this kind of purchase. But knowing something's for sale is a different matter.''

Peter didn't quite grasp the difference, but acknowledged it was business, not his thing. He had a third burning question. ''What's with that hat?''

''What?''

''The hat.'' When she still looked obtuse, he added, ''That dumb-looking hat he was wearing.''

''The *beret*.'' She grinned. ''It's the latest in hats, so that's just Jack being hip. He's always been cool.''

No one in Peter's life would ever call him cool, and he damn well knew it. How often had Mary Ellen called him innocent, naive or overall geek of the year? He didn't want to count.

He had only to look at her to see the sparkle of mirth in her blue eyes, the shapely figure, the long, auburn hair that made her such a stunner. *Hot. With it. Cool. And hip.* He couldn't forget hip.

So what was she doing with him?

And maybe she wouldn't be doing it with him much longer.

''I'm happy for you, Mary Ellen,'' he said, nearly choking on the words.

''Hell's bells, I'm relieved'' She sat back in the chair. ''Jack Crowley. Who would have thought?''

Not Peter Holiday, Peter admitted.

He hadn't seen this coming. Not at all.

OUTSIDE in the hoagie shop's tiny parking lot, Mary Ellen looked up at the sky. Stars twinkled brightly. The full moon looked down on her. Life was better and yet worse than the last time she had done this.

"Funny how it is," she said.

"I'm not laughing."

She glanced over at Peter and frowned. It occurred to her that while she had had a scare, he was still living his. "I'm sorry. I must have been like salt on the wound tonight."

He shrugged. "You weren't. I truly am happy your job's not threatened."

"Me, too," she agreed. "But don't you see? The work gods are looking down on us. I got the first break, that's all. You'll get yours."

"That's what I'm afraid of."

She put her hand on his arm. "I haven't thanked you for coming tonight. It means a lot to me."

"I shouldn't have spared the time. I really couldn't afford to."

She had heard her father say variations of the same thing to her mother—usually after he'd been nagged and made to feel guilty. Had she done the same thing tonight? She had an awful feeling she had. *Scary,* she thought. *Very scary.* "No, I can see you probably couldn't."

She realized they weren't the best words to say. She wondered if she could say something to correct them, but the moment passed.

"I'm glad you appreciate my situation," he said.

"I do." She knew his situation all too well. Peter wouldn't want to hurt her, but he wouldn't be able to help it.

"Good. I'm glad you understand."

Awkward silence ensued. Mary Ellen didn't know how to break it. Never before had she been so at a loss for words. She could feel the distance growing between them. The intensity she'd felt from the beginning hadn't lessened, but she was afraid she had seen Peter's true nature now with the crisis. She didn't want to change him. Changing people was never a solution to love.

She needed to protect herself, however, only she wasn't nearly ready to break it off with him, either. All this thinking, this weighing of actions, gave her a headache. She wasn't used to this sort of thing. Why couldn't relationships be straightforward? That was what Peter wanted.

"I need to get back to work," he said.

She could hear the underlying condemnation in his voice. "Thank you."

"For what?" he asked.

"For coming this evening. For listening. Will you be at my father's reception next week?"

He nodded.

"Good." She smiled.

He didn't kiss her. Instead, after another awkward moment, he got in his car and left.

Mary Ellen gazed up at the white moon. A lovers' moon. Tears blurred her vision.

She wished Peter would hurry up with his antidote for love. She had a feeling she needed it.

Chapter Nine

Peter stared at his drink, stared at the books in John Magnussen's library, ignored the small groups of people in the room and wondered what the hell he was doing here.

It was another reception at the Magnussen mansion, this time for John's birthday, with a Philadelphia Who's Who in attendance. But it was another chance at impressing those in charge of the grant, and another guaranteed gut-churning afternoon.

"Last time I got shot in the butt," he muttered, remembering his other visit to the Magnussen house. He downed a healthy gulp of his white wine. Drowning his troubles in alcohol wasn't wise, but the wine sure tasted good and it beat almost wishing he'd get shot again.

Only he hadn't seen Mary Ellen yet.

"Peter. You get rocked by the proposed cuts, too?"

Bill Underwood joined him. Another candidate for the grant, Bill studied the growth patterns of third-world populations and their impact on the global environment. He also had a small research center that had never quite gotten off the ground, despite being well known for the integrity of its work.

Peter normally would stay closemouthed with the other candidates, wanting to show no weakness. But Bill was a nice guy, one of the best. "More than rocked."

"Me, too. Think Magnussen knows?"

"Probably. Hell, Bill, I was in the newspapers with the senate-committee business."

"I thought that was more of an eye-blackener against the cuts than your being on the line for funding."

"They played it that way, but I'm on the line." Peter shrugged. "I guess I played it that way, too, for the media."

"Well, we've got some hope with the grant."

"One of us does."

"I'm taking advantage of the delay to strengthen my research."

"Me, too." Peter knew the extra time was to his benefit, to get more evidence that the antidote worked on an emotional response.

Talking with Bill reminded him of his obligations and true purpose. Fooling around with Mary Ellen was playing with fire. Besides, he wasn't sure whether he had any fire left to play with. Never had he seen anything go south so fast as his relationship with her. One moment she was wearing a mustache for him, and the next she was hugging some "old friend." He didn't understand how it had happened, especially when they had been building such an intimate friendship. Yes, they weren't truly compatible in some ways...yes, they weren't happy with the little time they could be together...yes, they weren't happy....

Peter had the sneaking suspicion he had answered his own questions.

Deciding to let it all go, he talked serious funding crunches with Bill. The house was crowded, people wandering in and out of the library, but he paid little attention.

Mary Ellen entered the room. His attention hit the ceiling.

She looked terrific in a blue dress. He hadn't seen her in days, and he hungered for her. Her skin glowed like cream, the light dusting of freckles on her arms endearing. A band held her hair back to fall in waves around her shoulders. Her gaze sparkled with mischief as always, and a smile hovered around her mouth. Her father stood with her, but that didn't stop Peter from admiring what he saw—or remembering her naked in his bed.

She glanced his way, her face lighting up for an instant as if she had been looking for him. Peter's heart swelled, pounding fiercely. His head spun. Then her features closed, a slamming of an emotional door. His heart stopped. His brain went blank. A shaft of pain pierced his soul. One look had made him ecstatic and the next had plunged him into despair.

How the heck did she do it?

"Peter..."

Bill recaptured his attention. They talked more, but Peter found his focus broken. Just because Mary Ellen had entered a room. Doubts crept in about their relationship and the other night. He hadn't talked to her since. Nor had she called him.

Had she ever found Jack Crowley attractive? Had she dated him before? She'd never really said no. Was he the man she'd been engaged to? Had she made love with him?

She better not have, Peter thought. He couldn't stand it if she had. Worse, was she attracted to the man now?

His antidote couldn't be ready fast enough as far as he was concerned.

Eventually her father made his way to them. Peter and Bill wished him a happy birthday. After Magnussen thanked them, he asked, "Enjoying yourselves? Need anything more?"

"No. Thank you, John, but no," Bill said, smiling.

"How about you, Peter?"

Mary Ellen stood next to her father. Her perfume, light and clean, swirled through his senses. He knew what he wanted, but he couldn't have it. Not anymore. "I'm fine, sir. Thank you."

Liar, he thought.

"I've hidden Mary Ellen's bow and arrows today, so you're safe," John said, actually smiling.

Peter grinned. He couldn't help himself and didn't want to. Magnussen had made a joke with him. That was promising. "I appreciate that, sir, believe me."

"Thought you might."

More people came into the library. Somehow, John and Bill became separated in the natural crush. Peter pressed close to Mary Ellen as someone brushed past him. Her arm rubbed along his chest. He felt deliciously burned.

"Are you having a nice time?" she asked.

"No," he said honestly. "I'm wondering why I'm even here."

She grinned. "You catch on fast. It might be a social reception, but Dad's sizing everybody up some more."

"I'm not surprised. We're all hurting with the proposed federal cuts."

He felt her stiffen next to him and knew he had

unwittingly brought up a bone of contention between them.

"What's wrong with us?" he asked.

"Lots of things, I think. You're a workaholic, like my father. I'm afraid I'll be a nag like my mother was. I've been one lately."

"It's just the situation, Mary Ellen," he said, realizing he was fighting demons he hadn't been aware of before. This was better than thinking she'd just changed her mind.

"Peter, you've told me often enough the center is your life's work—"

"Woohah! I feel great!"

Jack Crowley's entrance started a burst of laughter. The Keycast deal had been formally announced at a press conference on Friday, and Jack Crowley's "Woohah! I feel great!" pronouncement at the podium had made every local newscast for three days afterward. Peter had seen it several times, to his disgust. Somehow, revolted though he had been, he never quite got the channel changed before the sound byte played itself out to the end.

"Here's my girl," Jack said, coming up to them and putting an arm around Mary Ellen's waist. He kissed her cheek.

Peter felt a white-hot steam rise to his head.

Jack's arm stayed around Mary Ellen.

Peter thought his head would burst from the fury inside him. He wanted to rip Jack's arm away. He wanted to shout at Mary Ellen. Violence nearly overwhelmed him. What the hell was the man doing here?

"Peter, this is Jack Crowley, an old friend," she said.

Old friend, my arrow-shot behind, Peter thought murderously.

"Jack, meet Peter Holiday. He's a research scientist who's up for the Magnussen Foundation grant."

Jack towered over him. He had wide shoulders and a thick chest, clearly muscled even under his suit jacket. With a healthy tan, his muscles lithe and lean, he looked exactly the way a fitness guru should. Peter felt like the skinny kid getting sand kicked in his face at the beach.

"It's an honor to meet a scholar, man." Crowley stuck out his hand.

As if in a dream, Peter watched himself reach out and take Jack's hand in a gentlemanly handshake. He actually intended to be nice to this cretin.

The man squeezed his fingers in a grip of iron, nearly bringing Peter to his knees.

"Congratulations on your deal," Peter managed to gasp out.

"Thanks." Jack released his hand.

Peter felt the blood rush back into his hand, making his fingers feel like bloated sausages. He refused to let it show. "Mary Ellen was telling me about it."

Jack grinned. "She's great, isn't she?"

Peter stared at Mary Ellen, who looked far too comfortable snuggled in Jack's embrace. Everything inside him wanted to yell and scream and rip Jack's hand away. The damn thing was glued to Mary Ellen's waist. "Yes. Great."

"Holiday...Holiday..." Jack mused. "Are you related to Raymond Holiday?"

"He's my cousin."

"No kidding. I've known Ray for years. Damn, but

Jared Holiday was my wife's divorce lawyer. He cleaned my clock."

"He's another cousin of mine." Peter wished he could clean more than Jack's clock. "Jared's a bulldog for his clients."

"I'll say."

"His other cousin is the columnist, Michael Holiday," Mary Ellen said, rounding out Peter's family roster.

Jack laughed. "That guy's columns slay me, especially from his single man's point of view. My God, but you've got a crazy family. Peter Holiday...I swear I know that name in particular...."

That name. As if he didn't exist, Peter thought.

"Peter's well known for his behavioral work. He founded the Eastern Pennsylvania Research Center," Mary Ellen said.

Peter wondered if her praise of him was a good sign. He'd have to ask Michael. Although he preferred to let Jack twist in the wind, the man's next words surprised him.

"I knew I knew the name. Wow. That's terrific! I read your paper on eating disorders in *Scientific American*."

"You did?" Peter was surprised the man could read beyond Dick and Jane.

"Sure. When I was starting my first fitness center, I used a lot of it to counsel clients about their eating habits. Great stuff. Great stuff!"

"Jack's helped a lot of people to have a more positive, healthier life-style," Mary Ellen said.

"Hey. Life's too short not to enjoy."

Peter waited for "you only go around once in life" and other hackneyed expressions. He waited for Jack to take his arm from around Mary Ellen. It wasn't happening yet.

"This little girl and I are going to put basketball back on the map in Philadelphia. It's a great college-hoops town, but we've forgotten our roots...."

Peter ignored the rest of the lecture. He stared at Mary Ellen. She'd *said* she wouldn't be working with Jack. Jack had just said different.

"...I'm glad she's there for me," Jack said, giving Mary Ellen another hug. "I've always been half in love with her."

Peter felt the world go dark for one agonizing second. He squeezed the wineglass in his left hand. It didn't break. Too bad.

Mary Ellen had the nerve to laugh, actually laugh. Her gaze sparkled. Her face blushed prettily. "God, Jack, let me get the hipwaders out before you start throwing your bull around."

Jack laughed with her, a big booming laugh. He took her hand and, excusing them, pulled Mary Ellen away.

Peter just stood there, numb and yet mesmerized. He watched the two of them enter a heated discussion with three men he didn't know. He couldn't stop himself from watching.

Jack and Mary Ellen were a handsome couple. Both tall and graceful, they were beautiful representations of the male and female form. Peter had always been drawn to Mary Ellen's vitality. Jack matched her. The man radiated happiness, like a beacon illuminating the ocean depths. Peter knew the two were alike in mind and emotion. Jack would be a far better companion for her than a dour research scientist.

Maybe she already knew it.

Peter stilled. Only his insides swirled violently at the

thought. Maybe this was why she had been so funny and distant—especially lately. Maybe this was why she had been so stubborn about their lack of time together. Maybe her story about workaholics had been an excuse. She had found a man who suited her more than he, Peter Holiday. All the tensions and the coolness had been her way of letting him down easy. He might have thought it before. He might have, in his naiveté, given her the idea of how to break it off with him, now that the time really had come. She might have promised to tell him whenever she wanted to break it off, but maybe she subscribed to Michael's theory of allowing the "gracious" out. Maybe she was pushing him toward it first.

Peter stared at Jack. The man stood very close to Mary Ellen. Not even a ruler would fit between their bodies. Jack always seemed to touch her with his hands, too—her shoulder, her arm, her back. Peter knew Jack was marking her as his territory. And she didn't object. She didn't step away. She didn't tell him no. She didn't kick him where it counted. Nope. It was all clear to Peter now. Crystal clear. He had been betrayed.

Common sense told him to wait, and somehow he listened to common sense until he saw Mary Ellen alone. Jack must have gone to the bathroom. After blessing his Maker that the earthbound god functioned like a normal human being, Peter went over to her.

"Can I speak with you for a moment?" he asked, taking her arm. Without waiting for an answer, he led her outside, past the terrace, past the garden to the deserted tennis courts.

"We are getting brave," she commented. "This isn't good to be doing this, Peter."

"I'm not worried," he said, turning her to face him. "What the hell is Jack Crowley doing here?"

She looked startled. "Everyone from the mayor to the football-team owner is at this reception, or didn't you notice? Jack's a hot item right now, very visible publicly, and my father's known him for years, from when Jack worked at the center when I did. My father especially likes to strengthen ties to hot items, so I suggested he invite Jack."

"You. *You!*" Peter thought he would explode with anger. He couldn't believe this.

"What is wrong with you, Peter?" she asked. "We've barely talked to each other since the night you came to the center and now you drag me out of a reception to yell at me about nonsense."

"Why the hell is it nonsense when you're hanging all over that clown?"

"What clown? What are you talking about?"

"Jack Crowley! Jack Crowley!" Peter chopped the air with his free hand. "It's disgusting the way you hang all over the guy."

"I don't—"

"And he's hanging all over *you!*" Peter continued, not waiting for her protest. He was on a roll. "Could he stand any closer to you? I think not. Could he put his hands on you any more intimately? Only if you were naked!"

"Peter!"

"Don't deny it! It's clear enough! You've been with him and you want him again!"

"I do not!" Her outraged tone didn't appease him.

"Oh, yes, you do."

"Oh, no, I don't."

"Oh, yes, you do."

"Oh, no, I don't."

"How stupid do you think I am?" he asked. "Not as stupid as you think! You never hung all over me that way."

"You'd lose the grant, you idiot!"

"That's immaterial to this discussion." He pointed a finger at her. "You stay away from him, Mary Ellen. Or I'll—I'll…" He wasn't sure what he'd do, but he'd do it. "Just stay away!"

She stared at him, then gasped and said, "You're jealous! Really jealous."

Peter frowned, anger turning to confusion. "No, I'm not."

"Oh, yes, you are." She gasped again. "Peter! You're more than jealous! You're in love!"

He stared at her, his emotions a jumble inside him. "No."

"As a so-called wise person once said, take a pill, pal, and call me in the morning."

He felt galvanized into action. Only he didn't know what to do. Yes, he did. "No one should suffer like this. I've *got* to cure romantic love now!"

"No!" She grabbed his arms and shook him. "No, Peter. You're forgetting the other half of love. The tenderness. The protectiveness. The sharing. The courage. The giving."

"No."

She took his hand and led him away from the tennis courts and the house. "I've tried to show it to you over these past weeks because I knew just telling you to look at the good side of love wouldn't be enough. You had to *see* it. But we've had so many obstacles in our path that I haven't done a good job. Not as good as I would have liked. I have an idea. Come with me."

"Where are we going?" he asked.

"To see love."

"We'll be missed."

"No, we won't. The reception is due to break up anytime now anyway. We'll just have left a little early—if anyone notices at all."

At the estate garage, she put him in her car and drove him back into the city, to the Manyunk section with its trendy shops and restaurants. They would get his car later, she promised. They found a little café with an empty outdoor table. Mary Ellen settled him in a chair and ordered espresso.

"Now watch," she said.

As they sipped their coffee, he did. People strolled by on the sidewalk, taking advantage of the warm Sunday afternoon. Lovers, arm in arm, occasionally stopped and kissed, absorbed in each other and their feelings. Husbands carried packages and looked on with tolerant amusement at their spouses. Mothers and fathers hugged children, then walked holding hands. Wives indulgently nudged husbands caught looking at a passing pretty girl. Other wives and husbands nudged each other so as not to miss a pretty passing girl or a good-looking guy. Elderly couples strolled together, the wife's fingers tucked protectively in the crook of the husband's elbow, their love for each other still reflected in their gazes.

"Peter, if you're right about a chemical imbalance, you will kill all this," Mary Ellen said. "How do you know you will kill only romantic love? You could kill all love. It's a natural emotional response, and that's what you're against."

"But love hurts," he said in a low voice.

"It can. There's no denying it. Love isn't easy.

Nothing is easy. But to lose all this—the emotion that gives us hope... Peter, people need hope. People need to feel important in their significant other's life. You've talked about giving humanity a more productive, better quality of life. Just on that alone, love contributes tremendously to the economy. Where would florists be without love? Or the greeting-card companies? Or the movies? Who would sit in the balconies and neck? Who would go to the drive-ins and explore the back seats of their cars? The word *date* would vanish out of the vocabulary. Who would sing those silly love songs? What would be the point? So there go your music sales right down the dumper. And clothing manufacturers would suffer because no one would have a reason to buy a new outfit to look good for a lover, or to attract a stranger for love, or to impress a first date who might become their love. Everyone's bought tons of clothes for that. The economy would be a trade-off at best.'' She swept her arm around the café. ''All this happens today because of love. I say love has already taken us to the next level of civilization, Peter. Aren't we the only creatures on earth who experience love for a mate? Who mourn, maybe for the rest of our lives, when that love is gone? Some even pine away and die within a year or two after losing their spouse. If we didn't have that kind of love, then wouldn't we be like the other animals? Peter, you can't eliminate romantic love. You can't do it.''

He nearly agreed, her argument was so persuasive, especially in light of his own feelings for her. Then he noticed a small, self-serve newsstand. The newspaper in its little window blared the headline Man Kills Lover in 3-hour Police Standoff. ''What about that?''

He noticed other couples walking past the café. They

argued heatedly, unconcerned with strangers witnessing their anger. They said hurtful things. Parents yelled at misbehaving children. Old people sniped at each other from what was clearly long-ingrained habit. "What about all this, Mary Ellen? People are hurting themselves over love. I can stop it. How can you ask me not to? What if I were to turn like that—" he pointed to the news headline again "—because I love you? What if somehow I do?"

She stared at him, her face stricken.

MARY ELLEN WANTED to shake Peter, to smack some sense into his thick head. She wanted to laugh and cry. He loved her and yet his feelings scared him. Poor baby. She could have disabused him of his jealously over Jack, if she had known. On the other hand, because she hadn't, she'd discovered Peter loved her.

Still, she had to stop him from stopping love. Every fiber of her being demanded that she do so. Never had she felt such feelings before. Never.

"There's no denying that people can hurt each other over love and do."

"Then it should be stopped," Peter said.

"No." She took his hand again. "Peter, don't stop how I feel about you. I might as well be truly dead if you do."

"You love me?"

"Of course I do. I don't shoot men in the butt for nothing, even if Cupid might have helped me along the way." She squeezed his fingers. "Why do you think I acted so nuts when you didn't seem to want to find time to be with me? I'm not a fishwife for just anybody, Peter."

"I wanted to be with you. Every minute I want to be with you."

"I understand that now. I do understand about your having to work to save your center. I know now I would have done whatever it took to save my people's jobs, too, if it had come to that. My parents fought all the time, Peter. My dad's a driven man. Twenty-hour workdays are nothing to him. My mother wanted to be pampered and coddled by a twenty-four-hour-a-day husband. I think even now they still love one another, but they can't be together without destroying each other."

"See?" he said. "I could help them—"

"No. They have to change from within or let go. They let go. But I'm afraid we'll be the same. We already seemed headed down that road. Your work is more than a regular job, and I'm reacting to it just as my mother did to my father."

"It's temporary," he began.

"I know it is. Right now. But what if you can't stop working at this pace? It has its allure," she said with a lump in her throat. "I don't want to change you."

"Can you trust me?"

"Of course."

"Then trust me in this. I'm no workaholic, and you're not your mother. We will find a compromise. We have a good foundation in friendship, Mary Ellen. That will carry us further than romantic love ever could."

She wanted to believe him. She wanted to reach out and take what he offered, knowing it might be all she would ever get from him. "But love...Peter..."

"Trust me." He squeezed her fingers. Too tightly.

"Ouch!" she yelped, snatching her hand back.

"Okay, okay. I trust you completely. Anything to keep you from breaking my fingers."

"I'm sorry." He took her hand and kissed it, sending shivers down her spine. "Speaking of breaking fingers reminds me of Jack. What about him? He's all over you, Mary Ellen, acting as if he has some claim. Which he doesn't. Even if I have to punch him in the nose to get the point across."

"I like this possessive side of you," she said, grinning.

"I don't."

"It matches mine. I had trouble with two hot-to-trot students, remember?"

He grinned. "Oh, yes. I remember. I did get a warm feeling, too." His amusement faded. "I had nothing in common with those girls. They were kids, for goodness' sake! But Jack...anyone can see how alike the two of you are. You have so many things in common. Sports. Good looks. Athletic bodies. You are both so vibrant. I'm none of those things."

"We sound like a couple of rubber bands about to break," she commented, amused. "Yes, Jack's in my field of work. Yes, he looks good—"

"You didn't have to agree with me so fast," he muttered.

"Boy, are you in love. That's usually when people are at their most confused and insecure." She patted his hand. "It's understandable. You and I have more obstacles than most on the subject. Listen, Jack is a strong life force and very charismatic, but he's only ever been a friend. He does a lot of good, but he craves the spotlight too much. He can't deny himself the ladies. He is obsessed with success, bootstrap style. I could never put up with all that. I realized it long ago and I put Jack firmly in the friend category.''

''But he constantly touches you.''

''He touches everybody like that. Watch him next time you're around him. It's what makes him so good working with people.''

''He said he's half in love with you.''

She laughed. ''Jack says that to every woman. You should hear him with sweet little old ladies. You'd think he was a man too long on a desert island. He's always expansive, and he is good at motivating people to a more positive, healthier life-style. Without that expansiveness, he wouldn't be nearly as effective with others. But Jack as a mate?'' She shivered. ''I'd burn myself out in a day. I know it. You asked me to trust you. Now I ask the same thing. Trust me.''

Peter smiled, relaxing. ''Deal.''

Why had she ever thought his eyes were blue ice? They were as warm as a summer sky. His face was softer, too, less etched in sharp angles and more relaxed. She tried again to get her point about love across. ''You told me once that your father didn't marry for love. Are he and your mother happy? Truly happy?''

He thought for a moment. ''They're content with each other. They're friends. Yes, they're happy with each other.''

''Can you say their relationship has been exciting…like ours has been?''

''No.''

''We're in love. They're not. I can't imagine not feeling all the wonderful things I've felt for you…and maybe some of the bad, but it's all wrapped up together. I burn for you when you're not there, and I can't keep my hands off you when you are because I want to express how I feel to you all the time. Think about never feeling that again, Peter. Assure me that what your parents have is better.''

"I don't know if I can," he admitted. "But I know I can help people for whom love has gone wrong. How can I deny them that?''

She gazed into his eyes, feeling their relationship change to something deeper and more binding. Maybe she was making progress with him. Maybe he had a point, too. She put her discussion away for a time, and brought up another little problem. "We've agreed in the past to stay away from each other, and we sneak around. Now we know the truth—we're in love. This really puts your grant in danger.''

"I know." He kissed her fingers again. "It won't be much longer. It can't be. And then we can really be together.''

She hoped he was right. Yet she had very mixed feelings about him winning the grant.

Chapter Ten

Peter held the film up to the light, examining the scattered patterns of dots.

All the electrolytes and blood gases were normal. The enzymes were where they should be. An MRI showed a slight change in the electric patterns of the brain. But it was enough.

"Perfect," he muttered, tossing aside the delicate sheets of film. He wished he'd never seen them.

His theory was proved correct for the tenth time. A more-conclusive preliminary study hadn't been invented. Matthew had done a tremendous job of retesting the antidote. In fact, Matthew had handled most of the grunt work for years on this. Peter sighed, his feelings mixed. Certainly, he had enough evidence to convince the grant committee, and therefore Magnussen, that more study on permanently curing automatic emotional responses was warranted. For the first time, man could control irrational behavior caused by one particular emotion without affecting all the other emotions. And without side effects. His mice were healthy and happy. The physiology worked.

He really could stop romantic love.

What was that old Chinese proverb? *Be careful what*

you wish for. You might receive it. Well, he had wished—and received.

He thought about all the good he could do with the antidote. Troubled, hurt people would flock to it, having a cure, finally, for obsession and unrequited feelings. They *would* be happier, more productive. If only Peter's grandfather were still alive. He would be a happy man again, joking, laughing as he used to do, before his wife had found another man. Even his grandmother would have been happier. Both of them might have found contentment in the aftermath of tragedy.

Peter thought about Mary Ellen and what she had said about love. Had it already taken mankind to the next level of civilization? All those things she said about hope and caring and feeling so wonderful... could they outweigh that dark side of love? She said she loved him. He loved her. They had gone back to his place after their time at the café. Their lovemaking had held a tenderness that had seemed almost sacred. Peter wanted to experience it again and again with her. He wouldn't, if he took the antidote to avoid the pain being in love could cause.

He and Mary Ellen wouldn't take the stuff, he decided. But that showed no faith in his reasoning behind his work. He already had suffered some irrational behavior from being in love. Look at the way he risked people's jobs for a few stolen moments with her. His conscience demanded that he benefit from the cure. As the inventor, how could he not? Taking the antidote meant he and Mary Ellen would have a truly intimate friendship. Wasn't that better?

Yet what if Mary Ellen was right, and he killed more than the destructive powers of romantic love? A little voice inside his head warned him that *would* happen.

His research indicated otherwise, but he needed to do further testing on humans to know for sure. Much long-term testing. He needed the grant.

Later, in his office, he had a surprise visitor. For once, it wasn't Mary Ellen.

Jeremy Chelios sneered at Peter's diplomas and photos hanging on the wall. He took out a handkerchief and brushed off the perfectly clean visitor's chair before he sat. Peter gritted his teeth, but didn't comment.

"This place is a dump," Chelios pronounced. "I've seen better facilities in the middle of the Sahara Desert."

"Yes, I heard Yale had assigned you to their dumping ground when you were a graduate student. But I'm sure you didn't come here only to insult me—unless you're desperate. Which you probably are."

Jeremy smiled evilly. "Oh, I'm hardly desperate. I don't have to be. My work stands for itself."

"I hope the poor frogs can survive your work." Peter knew he should be above the nasty game, but he hated to seem as though he was intimidated. He vowed his next project would be a cure for jerks like Chelios. They really could be pleasant people underneath. He supposed.

"I ought to take you outside for that remark," Jeremy said, glaring furiously.

"Anytime." Peter stared calmly back. His rival outweighed him by forty pounds. Peter wasn't worried. He'd win easily, unless Jeremy managed to sit on him. Maybe that was his plan.

"I noticed you and Mary Ellen have become quite friendly," Jeremy said, completely changing the subject in a clear attempt to wiggle out of his challenge.

Peter refused to allow a muscle in his face to twitch,

despite the knot twisting his insides. "She's a nice woman and easy to talk to at receptions."

"You forget. I saw you kissing her at the Striped Bass. That was real easy talking, wasn't it?"

"What are you getting at?" Peter demanded, more than tired of the game.

"I saw you two driving away together from the reception the other day," Jeremy said.

"So?" Peter couldn't think of anything else to say. His brain scrambled for something more coherent. Nothing was there.

"So...where were you going, all cozy like that?"

"Hardly cozy," Peter replied. If Jeremy was asking, then he probably didn't know the answer. "Do you think if I were having an...*affair* with Mary Ellen, I would be driving in her car for anyone and everyone to see?"

Jeremy frowned. Clearly, he hadn't considered such an occurrence. That Peter was right didn't signify.

"If I'm not hiding, then there's nothing to hide," Peter added.

"I'm not a fool, Holiday—"

Peter burst into laughter.

Jeremy banged his palm down on Peter's desk. Furious, he said, "I'm not a fool! You're using the daughter and I have proof!"

"What proof?" Peter folded his hands on his desk. If he didn't, he'd wrap them around Chelios's neck. His mind screamed. *What proof? What proof!*

"I have it, don't worry."

"I'm not, because there's none to have." *Liar*, he thought.

"I'll give you a chance to save face, Holiday, because if this gets out it will ruin your reputation forever. You won't get a dime from *anyone*."

Peter smiled. He refused to show concern—or panic.

"You have two weeks, until the presentation, to withdraw your grant application. If you do, I'll give you the proof and I'll never breathe a word of it to anyone. If you don't, I'll go straight to John and *show* him how you're using his daughter to get to him."

"You're pathetic, Jeremy, if you think you can scare me with nonsense like that."

"You won't think so when you're out and I'm in."

"You're going to look like an idiot, Jeremy, because you've got nothing. I told you that once before."

"Can you bank on my having nothing? Can you *afford* to?" Jeremy looked around the office. "I hear not."

Peter knew his personal crisis had come to Jeremy's attention. It could have been Bill who'd told him. Nice guys often shared too much information. It could have been the meeting in St. Louis. Word of that had to be getting around general scientific circles, although it hadn't exactly been a secret, either. Or his appearance before the senate committee. Jeremy could have made a correct assumption for once in his life. Still, he had to be bluffing about the proof. He *had* to be.

Peter grinned ferally. "Don't believe everything you hear. Or see."

"We'll see." After emphasizing the threat, Chelios rose. "Remember what I said. Two weeks."

Peter took a parting shot. "Why not have a little faith in the merits of your own work? Or have you discovered you're really not the scientist you thought you were?"

"I have faith!" Jeremy exclaimed, looking ready to

explode. "But I also play to win. Two weeks, Holiday. Don't forget!"

He slammed out of Peter's office.

Peter sank back in his chair, feeling wiped. While he'd been dealing with threatened cuts in his center's funding and with superman Jack Crowley, Jeremy had been forgotten. But the snake in the grass had risen up and taken his bite when Peter least expected it. Or could cope with it.

The man had no proof, Peter firmly told himself. Why not just show it right then? If he did have it. Jeremy was bluffing.

He had to be.

MARY ELLEN GLANCED around, carefully surveying the parking lot in front of Peter's town house. No one was visible in cars, on the sidewalk or anywhere else. No one should be, she thought, the hour being well after midnight.

The lights were out in most of the houses. To her relief, one did glow in Peter's bedroom. She wouldn't have to break his door down to get his attention.

She parked the car, then glanced around again before finally being satisfied her original assessment had been correct. After getting out of the car, she crept furtively to Peter's front door. Her body tingled with excitement. She couldn't quite catch her breath. Her forbidden-lust theory was definitely kicking in.

No. Forbidden love.

Well, lust too, she thought. That was definitely in the mix.

"Now I'm arguing with myself," she muttered, ringing the doorbell.

All she knew was that she had been a very good girl

lately. When Peter wavered during the last two weeks, she had been the one to bark at him like a drill sergeant to stay in line. She had thrown herself into her work, not hard now that new management had come in. She had learned patience and compromise. She had made no snotty remarks about heavy workloads.

But she had missed him terribly. She just needed a little reward tonight for disciplined behavior. She just needed Peter's touch. She needed to express her love and to feel his newfound love for her.

The door flew open.

"I knew it! I knew..." Peter's outrage turned to astonishment.

"Like it?" She curtsied, spreading the green skirt as she did. "I thought the Girl Scout selling cookies was better than Lola—"

"Go home."

She gaped now. "What?"

"Go home! Go home before I drag you in here...oh, hell!" He yanked her almost harshly over the threshold and shut the door behind them. "You can't be here, Mary Ellen!"

"I know it's risky...." She narrowed her eyes. He looked almost scared. "You don't have those two students upstairs, do you? I'll kill you if you do!"

Peter waved his arms. "I'm serious, dammit! Chelios was in the office today, saying he had proof of our affair."

Mary Ellen stared at him. Words failed her for an agonizing moment. "Does he?"

"I don't think so. He refused to say, other than he saw us leave the reception in your car."

"What did you say to that?"

"That if I was in your car for anyone to see, then how could I be hiding anything?"

"Good answer." She opened the front door, saying loudly, "Thanks for buying the cookies, mister."

Peter shut it before she could depart. "Forget it. You're here, so the damage, if any, is done. Although I panicked when you came, I do doubt that he's out there lurking around like some spy."

"I'm so sorry, Peter. I never should have come."

"I'm glad you did."

He took her in his arms. Her head rested on his chest. She could hear his steady heartbeat. His warmth comforted her. She wrapped her arms around his waist and let herself be enveloped by his love.

"Where the hell did you get that outfit?" he murmured in her hair.

"In a costume shop. You never answered my question about whether you liked it."

"I don't know. Maybe if you had a mustache on..."

She hugged him tighter. Finally, she pulled away. "Let's go into the kitchen, have some coffee and stay up all night talking. That would put a crimp in Jeremy's proof. Besides, you better tell me about your conversation with him."

"You need to know."

In his kitchen, she found some instant decaf and made coffee. They both took sips of the hot liquid. Mary Ellen wrinkled her nose. "We probably didn't need to worry about caffeine if we're staying up all night."

Peter smiled wryly. His face looked drawn and haggard.

"Tell me," Mary Ellen coaxed.

"He came to see me this afternoon, late afternoon."

Peter chuckled. "Actually, I thought it was you at first. I think I've been unconsciously wishing you'd break down and come. You've been way too strong lately."

"So it was telepathy. I wondered about that." Ruefully, she added, "I should have been stronger, Peter. If I had known, I would have been."

"We won't know that for sure unless Jeremy comes out of the bushes, camera flashing. He says he has proof of our affair. He won't say what it is. He's given me two weeks to withdraw from grant consideration or he'll tell your father."

"Oh, no, Peter!" Tears stung her eyes. Panic shot through her body. She might not agree with his project, but she was playing fair, out in the open, to convince him he was wrong. But this... "That's despicable."

"It is. I told him he ought to trust the validity of his own work, rather than eliminate competitors in less-than-honorable ways."

"Logic is a lovely thing in the hands of a master," she said proudly. "You nailed him. Good for you!"

"I think he's bluffing," Peter said. "I think he's trying to push me into doing something stupid. If he's got something, then why not show it? I wouldn't withdraw if he did, anyway. I'm not ashamed that we love each other, although we have reasons not to flaunt it right now. But if it does get out, I have faith in my work, enough to let it stand on its own merits and defy being turned down for any other reason than a better project. If your father's got nerve to turn it down on less than that, then shame on him."

"You're right." She shook her head. "I've known Jeremy for years, although there's always been something smarmy about him for my tastes. If I know my father well enough, and I think I do, this won't endear

Jeremy to him, either. He'll wipe himself right out of the grant competition."

Peter smiled. It reminded Mary Ellen of cat-with-a-canary satisfaction.

"Good," he said. "If Chelios takes me down, then he takes himself down, too."

"Think if I pointed that out to him, he'd keep his mouth shut?" she asked.

"You stay out of this. It's between Jeremy and me."

"Now wait a minute. Who's the other half of this affair? Marge Simpson?"

Peter chuckled.

"I'm not allowing you to be hurt by some pompous jackass."

He took her hand. "Much as I appreciate your being ready to defend me, I won't allow you to sully yourself confronting Jeremy." When she opened her mouth to protest, he added, "No. Don't even think it. If you thought I was angry over getting shot with the arrow, let me tell you, that was mild. I'm asking that you respect my wishes in this. I know it's tough for you, but you can do it."

"You're taking away all my fun," she muttered.

"I'll accept that as a yes."

"I know!" she began, excited as a wild and crazy idea hit her. "Let's run away and get married!"

Peter's jaw dropped. He stared at her, saying nothing.

Mary Ellen faltered. "I—I just thought Jeremy wouldn't be able to shred our reputations if we were married."

"That would really make your father disqualify me. I'd be family then."

"Oh. Right. I forgot about that."

His common sense hurt her. They were silent for a moment. A long moment.

"Don't you want to marry me?" she asked in a small voice.

He hesitated. That hurt, too. "Do you?"

Suddenly she felt the same hesitation he did. "I love you, Peter, but maybe I'm not quite ready for marriage."

"But you were just ready to marry me."

"To save you."

"Oh, I'm savable but not marriable."

She chuckled. "Oh, Peter, do you hear yourself? You're angry with me for impulsive behavior *you* talked *me* out of. That's not logical."

"I suppose not. But I don't want to be logical about that."

"And I don't want to be impulsive." She sighed.

"I think we just want to be sure we have the right reasons for making such a big commitment."

"Jeremy's threat isn't it. Is it?"

Peter shook his head.

"So what is?" she asked, truly wanting to know.

"You're the expert in love. You tell me."

"We have to love each other," she began thoughtfully.

"We do, although I would argue more for our intimacy and friendship. They're great building blocks."

"You build your blocks your way, and I'll build them mine. Now. We also have to want to spend the rest of our lives together."

"I can't imagine being with anyone else."

That pleased her. "We have to make a commitment of faithfulness."

"I've already made that in my heart," Peter said.

"Not fair. I wanted to say that." She smiled. "We have to be willing to face the world with our love." Her smile faded. "I'm not willing to do that yet, for your sake."

"I want to, but I have all those people dependant on me."

She had no further qualifications. She agreed with him totally. "And the truth is, we're hopeful...but still getting to know one another. That's a good thing. If this is truly real, it can wait. It will be better for waiting."

"Out of the mouths of babes...and you are a babe. I know it's a politically incorrect thing to say, but have I told you that lately?"

"Not often enough." Mary Ellen lifted his hand and kissed it. "I have all this impulsive behavior now, and nowhere to go with it."

"Soon." He tightened his grip on her fingers, the pressure gentle and reassuring. "Tell me how things are going at work. Still staying away from Jack Crowley?"

She chuckled, amused by his jealous twinges. "Yes. Jack's been busy hiring new staff people for the team. I've been busy with the Keycast people. They really want me to push more women's sports in the arena. They have all these plans to broadcast them on the new channel. I think they want to go national with some of them."

"Great!"

"How about you?" she asked.

He shrugged. "We're all waiting to hear whether the budget passes with the funding cuts."

She knew he worried. He was on the edge of a precipice, and just her presence could push him over the edge into disaster. She shouldn't have come tonight. More than ever, she couldn't stay away. "I'm sorry. I put my needs before yours again, tonight."

"I asked you first about your work."

"No. I meant by coming here."

He ran his hand up her arms, sending shivers through her with his touch. "It was my need, too. I'm the selfish bastard who risks people's livelihoods to be with you."

"We are both selfish."

"I can't help it. I've never understood how I've lost all control over this relationship, but I'm not objecting."

"I know exactly what you mean," she admitted. "I love you."

"I love you, too."

They tightened their clasped hands. Peter's thumb stroked the fleshy pad of her palm. She wanted him with every fiber of her being, yet she was content to simply sit here with him.

"I have other news," he said finally, but he smiled.

"Tell me," she said, feeling it would be good. Certainly better than that creep Jeremy. What nerve! Too bad she had promised Peter she'd stay out of it. She would love to push Jeremy's nose in...

"My antidote is solid. Matthew and I have been testing and retesting it. It works."

Mary Ellen gasped. Her body went oddly numb. She knew without asking what he meant by antidote. She knew she should be happy for him achieving his goal. Yet everything inside her objected fiercely to such an achievement. "No."

He nodded.

"Destroy it, Peter. It's dangerous."

"How can you ask me to destroy my work?"

"I don't know. I don't know." She trembled as a cold chill slid up her spine. "It's wrong. Somehow I know it's very, very wrong. It's like—it's like the atom bomb. Because of the bomb's destructive power, we now live under the daily threat of annihilation by some gung ho idiot with access to the big red button. If he even sneezes…kablooey! There goes Minneapolis."

He laughed. "The world's not going to go kablooey, Mary Ellen."

"Yes, it will. Peter, it's dangerous to stop romantic love."

"It's dangerous to have it."

"You'll kill how we feel about each other," she whispered.

"No."

"Are you saying that somehow we'll survive it?"

He said nothing for a moment. "No."

"You're tired of me already, aren't you?"

"God, no!" He urged her up and around the table until she sat on his lap. He held her tightly, smoothing her hair with one hand. They sat together, silent. Contentment stole over Mary Ellen.

Peter said, "We would always have this, and this is good. Admit it."

"It is good." She raised her head and looked into his gaze. "But, Peter, you don't have this without the ups and downs that go with love. One does not exist without the other. It's nature."

"Something better might exist instead. That's the beauty of it. Happiness, satisfaction, respect, caring will all still exist. I'm only eliminating the obsession, the anger, the destruction."

"And passion," she added.

"I don't think so." He grinned. "I couldn't feel less passionate about you."

"Have you ever seen the yin and yang symbol?" she asked, desperate to make him see the truth of what he was doing. Never had he been more innocent than now.

"The circle split with a light side and a dark side? Yes, I've seen it. What about it?"

"The halves represent good and evil."

"I know that."

"Do you know what the small, dark circle means in the good side and the small, white circle means in the dark side?"

He frowned. "Not really."

"The light side, the good, must have a drop of evil within it to recognize the danger and thereby avoid its temptation. Evil, the dark side, has a drop of good within it so that it will always have an opportunity to find redemption. Without either, we would have no strength and no hope. The Chinese figured out the meaning of life over four thousand years ago."

"What's your point?"

"Listen up, big guy. This is important. My point is that love needs all its forms in order to be as wonderful and abiding as it can be. Without its dark nature, couples would not strive to achieve the promise of a more perfect relationship. They would simply mate and move on. Ultimately, people will be far more lonely with your drug than without it."

"No, they won't. People would only take the antidote to get over the pain or obsession. They would stop taking it after several months. It would work the same as Valium does for depression. It only dulls the emotions for a time."

"Valium is addictive."

"Physically. Thus far in tests, my drug isn't."

"Thus far."

"It's a very good thus far."

"It will be emotionally addictive. You'll see. Ka-blooey!"

He shook his head. "You don't understand. But I know it's because you're not a scientist. I don't expect you to grasp the potential. But Mary Ellen, I know I can help people with this."

She disentangled herself from his arms and rose. "Peter, you might be right about helping people, but I know I can't support what you're doing. What an awful thing I'm saying! I'm so sorry."

"I forgive you. I told you, you're not a scientist. I understand your skepticism."

"Well, I wish you'd kick me in the butt or something. I'd feel better."

"I wouldn't." He glanced behind her. "Your butt's too cute."

"You won't think that once we all start taking the drug."

"Oh, yes, I will. It doesn't affect the mating urge, believe me. I made very sure of that. In fact, the mice seem to be mating more."

"We're not mice!"

"We're better."

He reached for her but she evaded him, shocking them both with her rejection.

"I can't. I just can't!" she said, waving her hands, frantic to make him understand. Tears filled her eyes and choked her words. "I thought I could keep this separate. I thought our biggest problem would be the grant and having to sneak around. Now I know it's really this.''

She spun on her heel and ran out of the house.

Chapter Eleven

Phone calls did not work.

Flowers did not work.

Even one dozen red roses did not work.

"So much for love," Peter muttered, staring blindly at the mice in the large cage. Several pairs mated happily under his unfocused gaze. "She won't talk to me, fellows."

"Who won't talk to you?" Matthew asked. He had an armload of printouts and clearly had been on his way to his own desk when he overheard Peter's mumbling.

Peter straightened. "The mice."

"You said she."

Damn scientists, he thought. They always paid too much attention to details. "Well, I meant Sylvia the mouse."

Matthew peered in the tank. "No wonder Sylvia won't talk to you. She's pretty busy at the moment. Boy, look at Rochester go!"

"Forget the mice." Peter waved a hand. "What do you think of this? Do you think the suppression of romantic love is an opportunity for mankind to better itself? Or are we dooming the species to a zombie hell?''

Matthew frowned, obviously thinking. Peter hoped he didn't hurt himself. Finally, Matthew said, "Betterment. I know I can't wait to take it. Jill dumped me this weekend.''

"Sorry," Peter said, feeling bad for his assistant.

Matthew shrugged.

After his assistant returned to his own work, Peter wondered how much losing a girlfriend affected Matthew. Outwardly he seemed calm, although a bit more wistful, but he functioned well. The antidote probably wouldn't help someone like Matthew, anyway. It really was designed for the obsessed individual who was out of control.

Unfortunately, Peter was rapidly becoming his own best candidate.

He had to talk to Mary Ellen...but how?

With Jeremy breathing down his neck, he couldn't just go to her home or office. Even a disguise was too risky. He depended on the telephone—but she had to answer the damn thing for it to work.

She had proposed marriage. He had hesitated, feeling like the reasons were all wrong. Had he been a complete fool? He wanted more than impulsive behavior, but he seemed to have stepped into a pile of stupidity.

He stared at the mice, looking for clues that would tell him she was right about love. In classic textbook action of his theory, the little creatures snuggled together constantly, sleeping or no. They willingly shared their food, showing no territorial aggression about it or anything else in their environment. Not even the mating males fought over the females. They even seemed to wait their turn, as if one would say to the other, "After you, my good mouse.'' They had been on the final version of the antidote only a few weeks, and the behavior change was dramatic—happy, healthy mice living and loving together.

The potential for humans was tremendous.

Now if only Mary Ellen would take a damn phone call...

Two days later, she still had not answered his calls. She showed up instead.

He spotted her standing by his car when he left the center late one evening. Her hair hung loose, sweeping about her shoulders. Her mouth was compressed, tempting him to make it blossom with kisses. Her hooded sweatshirt and jeans only teased him about the body underneath. He knew it well, yet it held so many mysteries still.

Peter wanted to hug her—and yell at her, half of him angry that she hadn't contacted him before and the other half angry that she risked the grant yet again to see him. A little voice told him the math wasn't right on his halves, but he didn't care. She was here.

"The stars are really beautiful,'' she said, when he was a few feet from her. "Especially when you've got forty-five minutes to look at them like I have.''

"You were here forty-five minutes?'' he asked, momentarily distracted.

"I was trying to beat your record, but you came out too soon.''

"Why didn't you come inside?'' he asked.

She gave him a pointed look.

"Right,'' he muttered. "Well, no one's here now. Come in and have coffee.''

The air didn't feel chilly, for the late April nights

were generally warming. Still, she had been out here for quite a while.

She shook her head. "Thanks, but I won't stay long. Can we sit in your car? Or mine?"

"Sure." He unlocked his door and opened it. "This isn't really the best of neighborhoods."

"No one bothered me." She got in the car.

He shut the door behind her. The realization that she had been here alone bothered him while he walked around to his side of the car. Once he was in the driver's seat, he faced her and said, "I don't want you hanging out here like that, Mary Ellen."

She pulled a small canister out of her pocket. "I have my hot-pepper spray. I was all right."

"You might not have been—"

"Peter, I didn't come here for a lecture. Please!"

She looked upset, her eyes wide and anxious, her mouth turned down slightly. Her face looked drawn, but that could have been the parking lot's glaringly bright halogen lights.

"I have bad news," she said.

His stomach tightened. Whatever gulf lay between them suddenly didn't matter. "What's wrong?"

"I shouldn't be here," she murmured, suddenly turning away. "God will punish me for this. My father certainly will."

"Mary Ellen!"

"Oh. Right." She made a face. "I hate this. I had dinner with my father the other night."

"He found out about us," Peter said. Jeremy had had proof and shared it. An odd, invisible burden began to lift from his shoulders. He could actually feel it.

"No."

The burden smashed back down.

"Well, maybe..." she conceded, frowning.

The burden lifted again, yet hovered. Before he would go more crazy, he urged, "What? *What?*"

"He talked about the grant candidates." Mary Ellen reached across the console and put her hand on his arm. "He rarely talks about individuals, but he did that night. He mentioned he liked Jeremy's research. He thought it was timely and had merit."

"Okay," Peter said, trying to calm his concerns. "So he thought Jeremy had merit. God knows why, but he's entitled to his opinion."

"Peter, he didn't mention anyone else except in passing. Certainly he didn't say anything about what he thought of their grant proposals. And he didn't mention you at all."

Peter's insides flipped over. "Not at all?"

She shook her head.

"What do you think that means?"

"It means the man in the moon has a better chance at the grant." She fluttered her hand. "I shouldn't be flip at a time like this."

"I have the feeling you're not being flip at all," he said, taking a deep breath. "But why the hell would he like Jeremy's project best? There were several others whose work had more merit. Or so I thought. Bill Underwood has a very good project on population effects."

"It's probably the rain-forest angle. People are looking at that problem more and more closely. It's very worthy, don't misunderstand me," she hastily added. "But it's also politically correct and a media buzzword at the moment."

"Well, that's a silly reason to give someone a million-dollar grant."

"Our involvement with each other is an equally silly reason for you to automatically lose grant consideration, yet that's where we're at," she remarked.

"I hate it when you get logical." He stared at the research center in front of him. It had taken ten years of hard work to build it up to where it was. Now it was threatened because of a frog. Ironic.

"I'm sorry I don't agree with your work, Peter." Her voice sounded choked, as if she were crying.

He looked over at her. She *was* crying. "Hey! Don't cry, Mary Ellen."

She leaned across the console and buried her face in his jacket front. "I feel bad for you because I have no faith."

"I don't mind." He put his arms around her. "Really, I don't. I expect to have to prove it to everyone. I *should* have to prove it. That's science."

"Yes, but you shouldn't have to prove it to me. I should be the one person in the world who has total faith in everything you do."

"Oh, so if I were about to jump off a cliff because I hypostatized that I could fly, you would stand back and say, 'Way to go, Peter?'"

She giggled through her tears. "I'd lock you up on the funny farm."

"So why take my research on blind faith, too?"

"It's your work..."

"Doesn't matter. I think the best time I've ever had with you, outside of the bedroom where you make me go kablooey, is when you took me to Manyunk to try and prove me wrong. It was a great thing."

She raised her head. "It was?"

He kissed her. The tenderness of their lips together, questing and coaxing, rocketed through him. It gave him that incredible, unduplicated high that nothing on earth could match.

When he finally eased his mouth from hers, he whispered, "I don't want some puppet, Mary Ellen, to parrot me. You don't have to believe in my work if you don't want to. Just believe in me."

"Oh, Peter."

He grinned. "Did I ever tell you I love the way you say that?"

"No. Do you?"

"Oh, yes."

"Oh, Peter."

"You're turning me on."

"Good. I *do* believe in you," she said. "Even if I disagree, I know you will do what you think is right, what you believe will help people. You won't be doing it for money or acclaim or prestige among your peers, but because you feel it's the right thing to do, no matter how wrong you might actually be—"

"Watch it. I'm not *that* noble."

"Sorry." She chuckled, clearly remembering apologies were a problem spot between them. "I'll still work on changing your mind. That okay with you?"

"I wouldn't have it any other way."

"Good." She was silent for a moment, then asked, "What are you going to do about the grant?"

"Nothing."

"Nothing!" She gaped at him. "Peter, you can't do nothing! You've got to fight for it. If you don't, you'll definitely lose it. I can't believe I'm telling you this."

"You are a fair person, Mary Ellen. It's one of the things I most admire about you. However, if what you tell me is true, then it's already lost and no amount of fighting will retrieve it. If it's not lost, then I want my work to stand on its merits. I want to win the grant because people see the worth of my project as I see it. So I'll do nothing more than I would normally do.''

''But you've gone all-out over the proposed federal funding cuts.''

''I've been pushing, that's true. But it's to keep what I already have. I don't have the grant, and there are protocols involved in it. I'm staying within those protocols.''

''I think you should tell my father about Jeremy's threat.''

''I would have to tell him what Jeremy's threatened. I still don't believe he has any proof. He's the kind of guy to rub it in your face if he did have it, or take it to the authorities like a tattletale. If I were to tell your father what Jeremy threatened, it's only logical that your dad would get suspicious and begin snooping around himself. That'll be it for the grant, anyway.''

''Oh, who needs logic? Where did it get Spock?''

''Huge fame through a TV series and six movies?''

''My side's killing me from the console.'' She straightened away from him. ''Okay, so Spock did good. So will you, if you strike now.''

''You make this sound like a hit, and I'm the hit man.'' He shook his head, feeling confident about his reasoning. ''No, Mary Ellen. Every instinct tells me to let my grant stand or fall on its own merits. I have the presentation coming up—''

She clapped her hands together. ''That's it! That's the place where you knock 'em dead.''

''I hope not,'' Peter said. ''No one would be left to vote.''

''You're a regular Howie Mandel, poor thing.'' She

threw her arms around his neck, hugging him tightly. Too tightly.

Peter patted her arm to get her attention, while gasping, "Aagghh! You're choking me!"

She loosened her grip, but kissed him breathless, anyway. "The presentation's got to be dynamite! What can I do to help you?"

Fear ran down Peter's spine. "Don't do anything, Mary Ellen. Please!"

"But I want to help you," she said earnestly. "I need to help you, Peter."

He kissed her cheek, thinking furiously the entire time. He had to deter her. Mary Ellen throwing herself into a project was like a hippo throwing itself into a mud hole. Everything was bound to go *splat!* "I appreciate that. I really do. But what could you do to help me?"

"I don't know. Run errands. Type stuff. Pour things into test tubes."

"You have to be a scientist to do that. Besides, you don't agree with my grant, anyway. Why would you want to help it?"

"I want to help *you.*" But she paused. "I would be helping you to ruin love."

"You wouldn't feel good about that. For once, why don't you be the woman behind the man? *Way* behind the man. I know it's alien for you, but that's really the best way you can help me right now. Under the circumstances, it's really the only way."

"I suppose."

She sounded so disappointed, he almost reneged. Almost. He was no fool.

He stretched across the console, taking her back in

his arms. He tucked her head under his chin. "It's really for the best."

"You're so damn logical."

He knew disaster had been averted. Thank God.

As he held her, he became aware of the way her hair smelled like flowers on a summer's evening. Her skin was warm and soft. Her body tempted him, reminding him of how long it had been since they'd made love.

"Making love in a car must be an exercise in biomechanics," he said, even though he knew he shouldn't. Being together was a risk, more so now than ever before. That only enticed him all the more. "I'm just theorizing, mind you."

"Theory and practice could be two different things," she said, lifting her head.

"We really should answer the question. For mankind, of course."

"Of course."

He kissed her. She opened to him eagerly and he responded in happy Pavlovian manner. One kiss. He surrendered.

It worked for him.

MARY ELLEN TRIED to concentrate on her computer screen, but no sooner did she berate herself than the figures ran together again.

"Damn!" she muttered, knowing full well what was wrong with her.

Peter simply didn't grasp the problem about Jeremy and the grant. She knew her father, knew where he was leaning from the conversation they'd had, but it wasn't too late. Peter could sway him back with a little schmoozing and a lot of cage rattling. Something. Anything.

She knew Peter would go on in his stubborn, plodding way, insisting on science over attention-grabbing flash. Science was all well and good—but a little attention-grabbing flash wouldn't hurt science at all.

Even though she found his research about emotional responses, especially romantic love, dangerous, ultimately she would feel far worse not helping him than helping him. Hadn't Diana Lynn helped the president with Bongo? Hadn't Katherine Hepburn helped Cary Grant find his inner costa-clavicle? Hell, if it was good enough for Kate, then it was good enough for her.

Only how?

She still wasn't quite sure several nights later, when she sneaked into Peter's research center. Sort of sneaked. Peter opened the door for her.

"You really shouldn't have come," he said. "I shouldn't have allowed it…only I'm starving."

"And I brought dinner. *Just* dinner." She shifted the picnic basket she carried from one arm to the other, not only to emphasize her point but because the damn thing was heavy. "You can't be eating right with your schedule, so it's one place where I can help without feeling I'm betraying my own cause or making a mess of yours—"

"I hope," he muttered.

"Thank you very much."

He kissed her cheek. She smiled, then added, "If that turkey Jeremy even thinks he's going to give us trouble, he'll hear from me. And he won't say a word after. Trust me. He won't be able to."

"That's what I'm afraid of."

He took the basket, then took her hand with his free one. His fingers were warm and strong around her own.

"I am glad you came. I've missed you."

"Do you think we'll ever stop playing this Mata Hari stuff?" she asked.

"God, I hope not. It's fun," he replied, grinning for a moment. "Soon, honestly. The presentation's in two days."

"How's it going?" She knew he was working alone tonight, which was why she had come.

"Good. I'm really happy with the results I have, and I should be ready early."

"Is it concise? Logical? Of course, it's logical. You don't know how to be anything else."

"You make me sound deficient."

She grinned. "Not after the other night in the car."

He let go of her hand and rubbed her back. "Nothing's finer than proving a hypothesis right."

How many more times could they risk being together without getting caught? Even midnight picnics could come crashing down on them.

Yet she considered it an opportunity, the last maybe, to show him how beneficial love could be. That was another reason she risked coming here tonight.

In the lab area, she laid out the red-and-white-checked cloth across a workbench. She lifted items out of the basket, saying, "I have ham-and-cheese sandwiches, chips and fruit. Soda for drinks. I thought of wine but I figured you didn't need to be drunk to be easy."

"Just put on a mustache and I'm there."

"I thought so."

He went into the men's room to wash up. Mary Ellen gazed around at the conglomeration of test tubes, beakers and Bunsen burners. It all reminded her of the old Mousetrap game. She looked in the real mouse cage, surprisingly large and spacious.

"These guys look happy," she commented to Peter,

when he joined her. "Oh, boy! Two of them are getting frisky."

"They're on the antidote."

Mary Ellen glanced up at him, gaping. "You're kidding!"

Grinning back, he shook his head. "No. They've been on it for several weeks, and the earlier version before that. This last batch..." He patted the flat of his hand on top of the tray of test tubes next to the cage. "This was the stuff that put them over the top."

She looked back at the snuggling, mating mice. "They have an—an aura about them, like they're radiating contentment."

"I know. I can't believe it, either," he said.

"This isn't what I thought would happen," she murmured, confused by what she saw. "Is there any down effect?"

"Well...like I said the other day, they mate a little more than before."

"And that's a bad thing?"

He chuckled. "Not hardly. I mean, it's not excessive and certainly not aggressive. They're eating and sleeping well. They're very alert and passing the normal behavior and intelligence tests as they had before. Their bio workup is excellent. The only side effect is that they mate more."

She giggled. "What a way to go."

"They're not complaining." He drew her away from the cage. "You're here. I'm starved. Let's eat."

They chatted while they ate, neither of them bringing up underlying worries. Mary Ellen kept glancing over at the cage, mesmerized by the results of Peter's work. Unexpected results. She just couldn't believe what she was seeing—happy, healthy, alert mice living a utopian existence. Had Peter actually found that elusive place?

"I can't get over it," she said finally, going back to the mice. They were still acting as though they'd discovered Nirvana. "They really are happy. Very happy. Those four just switched partners."

"Switching sexual partners is common in mice, although the males will usually fight about it."

"And these guys aren't fighting?"

"Not once. They've been real gentlemen and ladies, too."

She went over to the cage and peered in again, fascinated. "Are you sure they're not going to be sexed to death or anything?"

"No. The others would be mating, too, if they were. But they're sleeping and eating. It's not nonstop, believe me. Just a bit more than we normally see."

"Lucky things."

He came up behind her and ran his hands down her arms. "I think I'm luckier."

She turned to face him. Her breasts were against his chest. They were hip-to-hip, intimately hip-to-hip. His one leg pressed suggestively between her own. "Why are you luckier?"

"Because you're here."

He kissed her. Melting against him, she wrapped her arms around his neck. His mouth burned like a deep, rich fire. Her head swam. Her body ached. She was willing to do anything, risk anything, just to be with him.

They kissed again and again. His hands roamed her body. She plunged her fingers through his hair.

"Is love really like this?" he whispered against her lips. "I can't get enough of you. I can't control myself. I say one thing and do another."

"Bingo," she murmured. "I feel exactly the same. Why would you want to cure this?"

"I don't know. I don't know."

He kissed her again, then took her to the floor. After a moment, she didn't care about the cold, hard tiles under her body. She didn't care about the risks. Like Peter, she could no more control herself than he could. She'd known it when she had brought dinner. *Just dinner.*

To hell with it, she thought. She'd have dessert.

"Do you suppose all the action in the cage put something in the air?" Mary Ellen asked, gazing at the mice again. They were all sleeping in a pile of little, furry white balls.

Peter chuckled. "I don't think we needed any help getting turned on, do you?"

"No," she said, smiling. "Love is lovely, don't you think?"

He grinned wryly. "You're never giving up, are you?"

"Not me."

"Don't forget the mice. Maybe that has its place. It looks as nice as love, too."

She peered at the cage and the happy mice. "I admit it's got me thinking that you might really be on to something."

"Then let me have a crack at it. Think of all the people who would be helped by feeling like the mice."

"Maybe," she conceded, wondering if he was right. As a scientist, he did have some smarts she didn't. "I should go. You still need to work, don't you?"

"I was pretty much done by the time you arrived," he said. "Let me walk through the building to make sure everything's closed down properly, and I'll go out with you."

"I'll clean up the rest of the meal," she said, nodding.

He kissed her and left. Mary Ellen put the remnants of the dinner back in the basket. She went to the cage afterward, looking down yet again at the mice.

They seemed to mock all the things she had thought about Peter's experiment. If she could believe what she saw, Peter had done something astonishing. Its potential for the world could be absolutely tremendous in controlling emotional responses. But her father had already dismissed Peter out of hand—or he was close to doing so.

Maybe he needed to see what she had seen here tonight.

"We must have been born in the Show Me state," she muttered. But she liked the idea.

Only how could Peter show her father?

Mice just weren't dramatic enough for skeptics, and her father was clearly skeptical. If he wasn't, he would have mentioned Peter as the leading candidate. Peter needed something spectacular to showcase his research. He also needed something to ensure that Jeremy's threat, whether valid or not, fell on deaf ears.

Only how could she help him?

Her gaze shifted from the cage to the tray of test tubes and bottles. Peter said they contained the drug the mice took. Peter said they had no side effect—except for an increase in making love.

An idea burst full-blown into her head. Dramatic. Spectacular. Of bombshell proportions.

Impulsively, she reached out and took one of the tubes.

Chapter Twelve

"Do we have everything?"

Even as he asked, Peter frantically shoved around the boxes and audiovisual equipment being loaded into the van. He tried to count the materials. His brain couldn't function past the number three.

Matthew's hand clamped around his wrist. "It's all there, Peter. Relax."

"I can't," Peter muttered.

Mary Ellen had been with him two nights ago, but now he wished it had been last night. Never had he needed her warmth and cheerfulness more than in these hours before his presentation.

"Magnussen's a bastard, making everyone jump through hoops like this," Matthew commented.

"Magnussen probably wants to be sure that people are thoroughly committed to their research," Peter said.

"Can't he just give the money and forget it?"

"It's probably not as much fun," Peter replied, thinking of Mary Ellen's philosophy about things. Magnussen just had a sadistic streak to his "fun."

"Well, I think you guys ought to get together and

demand he just make a decision." Matthew slammed the van door shut. "Why put up with all this twice?"

"That's life," Peter commented, although Matthew's harping grated on his nerves. Probably because he felt like doing exactly what his assistant suggested.

Matthew still grumbled all the way to Temple University's science auditorium, site of the presentations, yet Peter felt a little better. Not relaxed, just better. Scheduled to go on last, he deliberately waited so as not to have to sit through the other presentations before his. He would have made himself insane with last-minute changes after seeing the others. No, going in blind was best.

Inside the building, he discovered he would be blinder than he'd originally thought. The auditorium stage was lit, leaving the audience in near darkness. It effectively hid the committee from the presenter's eyes. *Hell*, Peter thought. They could all be in the bathroom and he'd never know.

Maybe that was good.

As Matthew set up, Peter saw Bill Underwood in the back rooms behind the stage proper. He asked Bill how he did when he had been on earlier, but could tell from his hangdog expression the presentation hadn't gone well.

"I wasn't as sharp as I should have been over the questions," Bill said.

"You were nervous. You were probably better than you think," Peter replied. *What a damn shame*, he thought. Bill's project was terrific and really deserved funding. Peter realized he probably ought to be happy with Bill's misstep because it meant his own chances would be better. He just couldn't feel that way, though. He wouldn't even want to.

"Good luck," Bill said.

"Thanks."

His next encounter wasn't quite so magnanimous. Jeremy Chelios caught him alone in a back corner.

"This is your last chance to pull out of the grant, Holiday," he said.

"Stop dreaming," Peter replied. "I'm not withdrawing now or whenever your two weeks are officially up, which isn't today."

"You're a fool. You have no chance, and when the committee finds out you're romancing Mary Ellen, they'll dump you so fast you won't know what hit you."

"Leave Mary Ellen out of this," Peter said, growing angry with this twerp of a man.

"You dragged her in."

Jeremy still mentioned nothing about what proof he had. Peter decided to push the issue. "If you had proof, you'd be shoving it in my face right now," he said.

"I have it," Jeremy replied, drawing himself up haughtily.

He snorted. "So you claim. Prove it. Now's the perfect chance to prove it."

"I'm giving you an opportunity, Holiday. Be grateful and take it."

"You're hardly noble, Jeremy. Just remember, the moment you say anything about me, Magnussen's going to cut you off from the grant, too. He won't like you using his daughter to further your own ends."

"I am not!"

"Of course you are. He won't appreciate your making pictures of his daughter public."

"I don't have pictures."

"What *do* you have?" Peter asked.

Jeremy clamped his lips shut and just glared, obviously not about to be trapped further. Despite the opportunities he and Mary Ellen had given Jeremy, Peter knew now the man had no hard proof. Only some pretty fair guesses. After today's presentation, they wouldn't matter.

Peter pushed his face practically in Jeremy's. "You bring Mary Ellen anywhere near this and you won't ever live it down."

"You're threatening me!" Jeremy exclaimed, actually looking shocked.

"A threat for a threat. A promise for a promise." Peter decided to push it, to get an answer once and for all. He grabbed Jeremy's arm. "Come on. Come right on stage with me now and tell them what proof you have."

"No!" Jeremy shook him off.

"Fine, then I'll go out there and tell them about your claim."

"No!" A myriad of emotions crossed Jeremy's face, fear uppermost.

"I'm going to tell them," Peter threatened. "I'll make it my opening statement."

"All right! I thought I could get you to withdraw on a threat. Don't tell Magnussen, okay?"

"You're a weasel, Jeremy," Peter said. "Don't mess with me ever again. You won't like the results."

He walked away, leaving Jeremy sputtering. But the man should have gotten the point. He better have. Still, the confrontation had invigorated Peter, rather than causing more anxiety. He felt confident now. He felt strong, like Superman.

He felt himself being yanked into a closet.

Mary Ellen kissed him soundly on the mouth before whispering, "Good luck."

"What are you doing here?" he whispered back, astonished to see her. Brother, if Chelios could see him now.

"I've been here all day. My father thinks I want to get more involved in the foundation, so I'm observing the presentation. Jeremy's was terrific, I hate to say."

"Don't tell me that," Peter muttered, his self-confidence deflating like a popped balloon.

"You'll do just great. Believe me, I know." She kissed him again. "I better get back. My father thinks I went for a drink of water. Good luck!"

She slipped out of the closet and was gone.

After another stunned moment, Peter let himself out of the closet. He came face-to-face with Jeremy. The man grinned wolfishly, as if he'd just found a rabbit in a trap. Peter narrowed his eyes, silently sending his own challenge back.

"Dr. Holiday?" a voice said over a loudspeaker. "Whenever you're ready."

With a last glare, Peter walked on stage. The lighting left him feeling as if he was talking to thin air. His emotions urged him to change everything, because his planned presentation couldn't be good—or better still, pack it in because the odds were all against him. His logic told him to stay with his original presentation. Well, he'd preached long enough about the merits of his research. Now he'd find out.

Peter began the presentation. He had decided to take the committee through the life behavior patterns of animals, eventually working up to the point of human emotions and the effects of them on behavior. It had seemed the most logical and ultimately efficient way to bring them up to speed on his research. The slides and charts emphasized his points. He knew he was making the best presentation he could. He showed all he had on his first breakthrough about the emotion of romantic love and its antidote, emphasizing the evidence to point out the possibility for a broader breakthrough if more money were available for further studies and testing.

He also knew it was not enough.

"And in conclusion, ladies and gentlemen," he said, while silently preparing himself to make up on the questions, "mankind is held captive by the chemicals our own body produces—"

"Yes, we are!" Mary Ellen announced, walking boldly onto the stage. She carried a bow, an arrow notched on the string. She shot the arrow toward the ceiling where it stuck with a *thonk* to a tile.

"What the hell are you doing, Mary Ellen?" Peter demanded, at the same moment her father's disembodied voice did.

"I'm proving your premise," she said to him, while ignoring her father, who was somewhere in the darkened audience.

"By trying to shoot someone else with an arrow?" he asked, taking the bow from her.

"It was a metaphor for our first meeting and the significance of Valentine's Day on your theory about love. Peter, just give me—"

"You're supposed to be in the bathroom!" her father exclaimed, his voice close in the gloom. "Someone turn on the damn lights!"

The lights came on, turning the auditorium glaringly white.

"Okay. What the hell is this?" Magnussen asked, coming onto the stage.

"Yes." Peter took her arm. "What is this?"

Mary Ellen shook him away. "They need to listen to you, Peter, but words are not enough. Dad, Peter might really be on to something with this chemical imbalance. I saw it with my own eyes the other night."

"Ah, ha!" Jeremy exclaimed, pointing a finger at Peter.

"What other night?" John Magnussen asked, frowning.

"I can explain, sir," Peter began.

"I was at Peter's research center."

"Mary Ellen," Peter said, warning bells clanging in his head.

"You might as well have it all, Dad."

"I might as well hang myself from the rafters now," Peter muttered.

"I love Peter, Dad."

Peter looked heavenward. "Here it comes."

"You what?" Half the room gasped, along with her father.

"I've loved him from the moment I saw him."

"You shot him in the ass the moment you saw him!" her father said.

"Good point," Peter agreed.

"I shot him *before* I saw him," Mary Ellen corrected.

"That is true," Peter admitted, then realized it was a moot point. "Sir, I can explain. Mary Ellen, this is not the time for whatever you're doing."

"Yes, it is," she insisted. "I love you, but we can't be together because *you*—" she pointed to her father "—will immediately disqualify him from the grant."

"There's a conflict of interest," her father said.

"Poppycock! You're not in love with Peter. *I* am."

Good thing, Peter thought. He didn't know what she was up to, but it boded no good. "Mary Ellen—"

"Peter's received threats about how he should withdraw from consideration because of our relationship," she continued, then turned and glared pointedly at Jeremy, who shrank. "I won't have him subjected to that."

"But you just did!" Peter exclaimed in exasperation.

"I know, Peter. But we've hidden long enough, and there's a point to this, anyway." She turned to her father. "Dad, because of your antiquated notions—because of your conventional philosophies and ethics—I'm afraid you won't give Peter proper consideration for the grant."

"Well…"

"You need a demonstration."

"I do?"

"He does?" Peter repeated, becoming alert.

"Yes, he does. With Peter's cure for romantic love, people can be more productive members of society. I'm in love. I've done crazy things. I haven't been able to control my behavior—"

"You never could control your behavior," her father interrupted.

"But it's really bad, Dad. I've put Peter's grant at risk because I can't stay away from him. I've kept him from doing his job properly. I certainly haven't done mine right lately. All I want to do is be with Peter. In his arms. In his bed."

"Mary Ellen!" Peter yelped, horrified with how far she was going.

"I certainly don't want to hear this!" her father said, looking furious.

"I've caused Peter nothing but pain and embarrassment—"

"Now wait a minute," Peter protested.

"But with Peter's antidote..." She held up a test tube she took from her blouse pocket. Everyone stared at it. "I'll no longer be in love. I'll be cured."

Peter leapt toward her. "Mary Ellen!"

She twisted away. "You need to see what you'll miss without love, Peter."

She pulled off the test-tube lid and got the vial to her lips before Peter knocked it out of her hands and sent it shattering to the floor.

"Call 911!" he shouted. He cursed at being too late to stop her.

Mary Ellen gaped at him. "Call 911? But I thought this had no side effect!"

Peter grabbed her and began to hustle her toward the nearest bathroom. "I don't know what the human dosage is! Dammit, Mary Ellen, how could you do this? Quick, someone get syrup of ipecac! We've got to make her vomit."

Mary Ellen shrieked. "Peter! I barely tasted it!"

"You're crazy!" he said, furious with her. They weren't getting to the bathroom fast enough to suit him. "This was so foolish."

"But I love you."

"I love you, too, but you don't see me OD'ing on untested drugs to prove it!"

"But I didn't. Besides, you said—"

"I know what I said," he yelled. "And I don't give a damn. You better not die on me, Mary Ellen, or I'll never forgive you."

"But—"

He shoved her into the rest room, then into a stall. He'd cure her. And then he'd kill her.

GROGGY AND SORE, Mary Ellen sat up in the hospital bed. She had been poked and prodded by so many doctors that she thought she'd been plunked in a sea of them. Not a damned one had listened to her protests that the stuff never got beyond her teeth.

"Damn," she muttered, rubbing her throat.

She had had her stomach pumped, thanks to Peter. Her plan had been dramatic all right, straight out of "ER." She was as healthy as a horse—which she could have told them all if she'd been given a chance to do so.

The hospital-room door swung open and her father walked in.

"Damn," she muttered again.

"I should have known you didn't have an interest in the foundation," her father said, coming over to the bed. She didn't have to hear the words to know he was angry with her. He radiated it. "How are you feeling?"

"Thanks for asking that first," she said, glaring at him.

"Oh, no. You're not putting parental guilt on me, girl. I'm not the one who disrupted a scientific presentation to swallow God-knows-what."

"Maybe the next step for mankind, if only you'd get off your pedestal."

"You've made a real mess, girl. You know that?"

"I know," she whispered, hanging her head. "I didn't mean to fall in love with Peter. I honestly didn't want to at first. Neither of us can explain how we managed it, believe me. We've tried to resist each other. We truly have. But we can't.''

Her father said nothing for a moment. "I guess you do love him, because nothing else explains it. He's a steady guy, although a little offbeat, maybe, in his thinking. But that's what makes a great scientist. They don't think like normal people. They take leaps of logic to read conclusions and then go out and prove them right. You…Mary Ellen, I love you, but you just leap.''

"I thought Peter's demonstration needed some oomph, to really get your attention. You were talking about Jeremy's project far too favorably.''

"I was just talking.''

She eyed him. "You never just talk.''

He shrugged.

She sighed. "How long am I in here?''

"Holiday has you in overnight. You sure you love him?''

"Yes, I'm sure.''

"You could do a lot worse," her father said.

She took a deep breath. "The fact that I love him is why I wanted to take the antidote. I've caused him a lot of problems because I do. I have to admit, I also wanted him to see what being without love would be like.''

"You think his stuff really works?''

"Dad, I thought he was nuts the first time I heard his theory. I even tried to talk him out of it, because I thought eliminating love was dangerous to mankind. We've talked a lot about the hurtful things love also does, and then I saw the mice in his lab. They'd been on the antidote, and they were happy, not aggressive, cooperating with each other. I still have my doubts about what might happen without love. I don't want to lose this feeling I have for Peter. But the mice were impressive. Really impressive. The only side effect was that they mate more often—''

''And you took it! What the hell were you gonna do on that stage? No, I don't want to know.''

She chuckled at his outrage. ''I doubt that would have happened, not with the minuscule amount I half swallowed. If anyone bothered to listen to me. At least, I don't think it would have happened that fast.''

He rolled his eyes. ''Still, for you to just take it like that...''

''Peter said it was safe.''

''I talked to him, and what you took was not for oral consumption,'' her father said. ''What if you managed to down the whole thing?''

''I wouldn't have.'' She wasn't that dumb.

''You know medicine should be taken in a controlled way. This stuff...I'm glad Holiday acted so quickly. You're all I've got.''

She smiled and took his hand. ''Thanks, Dad. I love you, too. Dad?''

''Yes.''

''Don't disqualify Peter because I'm involved with him. That's so unfair, and ultimately harmful to the foundation to base its decision on something less than merits of the application.''

''There's a family connection that could be construed as unethical.''

''There isn't. All I'm asking is that you decide only on the basis of the work and its ultimate benefits.''

''You said he was being threatened. Should I disqualify that guy? Seems to me I should.''

Mary Ellen considered the question of Jeremy Chelios for a moment. ''No. Let his work speak for itself as well. If it's truly the most valid and has the most benefit to the world, then his project should get the grant.''

"I'll think about it. No promises.''

Mary Ellen wanted to argue the point, but refrained. She had done enough damage as it was. "I know you'll do the right thing, Dad. I trust you.''

"There goes that parental guilt again.''

"This time you need a dose of it.''

Her father laughed. "Okay. You made your point. On merit alone.''

"Good.''

Peter came in shortly after her father departed. He didn't take a seat, but stood next to the bed. He stared at her. His face was so handsome and so angry that she couldn't look him in the eye. Angry males seemed to be her lot today. Well, she'd caused enough uproar to deserve it.

"I'm so sorry, Peter,'' she said finally, in a low voice.

"You ought to be, after scaring the hell out of me like that!'' he said. "You just can't take untested substances. They have to be refined for human consumption. You could have killed yourself today.''

"Please, Peter. I don't need a lecture.''

"The hell you don't! I could have lost you. Do you know that? What would I do then?''

Mary Ellen cleared her throat. "Does this mean you're not as mad at me as I think?''

"Hell, no, woman!''

"Oh, Peter, I wanted to help you, to really show them what you and your research could do.''

"Next time you want to help me, tell me so I can

tie you to a chair, muzzle you and lock you in a cage, Hannibal Lecter style—''

''Oh, that was a really good movie, wasn't it? Especially when Jodie Foster was going through that dark house—''

''Don't try to change the subject,'' he said.

''Well, you did bring up Hannibal Lecter—''

''Enough!''

She opened her mouth.

''Enough!''

She clamped her lips shut.

''The entire presentation is a shambles.''

She nodded.

''I'm probably disqualified.''

She shook her head.

''I'm not?''

She nodded.

''I am?''

She shook her head.

''Dammit, Mary Ellen! Will you talk to me?''

''But you said not to.''

''Just answer the question.''

''I'm only pointing out—''

''Mary Ellen!''

''You're not disqualified. My father's agreed to judge the work alone, not any other connection. Including Jeremy's stunt. Including me.''

Peter gazed at her. ''You're kidding.''

She smiled. ''It seems the fiasco at least has my father taking a reasonable tack.''

''So we can see each other for the rest of the time?''

She scratched at the hospital blanket for a moment, suddenly feeling shy. ''Do you still want to see me?''

"The scariest thing today is that you wanted to kill our love."

She glanced up at his anxious features. "Oh, Peter, no! I never *wanted* to kill our love. I wanted to prove your theory right to my father and the committee. What better way than by someone who is in love and acting crazy because of it?"

"I can think of a million." He sat on the edge of her bed, then leaned forward and kissed her tenderly. His lips held passion and gentleness, the things she had risked today. He pressed his cheek against hers and said, "Don't *ever* do that again, okay?"

"Okay."

"I love you."

"I love you, too."

They kissed again. She put her arms around him and held him quietly for the longest time.

"Did you *have* to pump my stomach?"

He chuckled. "Absolutely."

"And all those doctors. Where did you find them all? At a local medical convention?"

"This is a teaching hospital. It's swarming with interns and med students."

"They all acted like I had some rare disease."

"That's because I acted like you had."

She sighed. "The first night we can openly be together, and I'm stuck in the hospital."

He kissed her nose. "Serves you right."

"Has the foundation rescheduled the presentation?"

He lifted his head. "Don't even think about a repeat!"

"Okay, okay. I'm just asking." She meant it. She was only curious about the aftermath.

"I'm not sure," he said, although he looked suspicious. "But I do know they intend to reschedule my presentation. Your father told me that the committee feels that's only fair."

"Good," she said, pleased he would get a second chance. Another idea formed in her head. "You know, Peter, you really do need something more than mice—"

"Mary Ellen, don't even think it! I forbid it."

"I have to," she said. "*You* have to, if you want to win the grant."

"No."

"Yes. Mice don't have the same emotions as humans do, and that's the heart of your research. Pardon the pun. You need a preliminary study of someone in love and acting foolishly and destructively. You need to show it *does* affect humans."

"But not you."

She gazed at him, saying nothing.

"You just promised you won't do this again!"

"I'm a prime candidate, and the committee found that out big-time."

"You *do* want to kill our love."

"No." Tears rushed into her eyes, surprising her. "No. I love you so much, I do want to help you. I admit I also want you to have a demonstration of what it would be like without our love. Maybe you'll finally see the two sides more clearly than you have been. What if you've been right all along, and I'm wrong? If the mice are any indication, then you are. I have to admit that the mice are giving me some second thoughts. If I take the antidote in a controlled way, afterward I should be productive and content. I won't be behaving outrageously. My father will like that. So will you."

"No. I don't want to change you."

"Peter." She grabbed the lapels of his jacket. "Listen to me. You have faith in your research, don't you?"

"Yes."

"Then you have to believe that you and I will be better people, happier with each other by *not* being in romantic love. I still believe eliminating love is dangerous. Our being without it for a time could prove one of our theories. For you, I'm willing to risk losing our love. How can you say no?"

He pulled her against him. "I can and I will."

"Peter, think. You can't pick and choose volunteers right now. You're in a major crunch. If you want to save your research center, you need me to do this. I *need* to do this. I love you. I want to help you if I can. This will, one way or the other. If you're right, we'll still be happy and content with each other, like the mice are."

"What if I'm wrong?" he asked.

"Then we'll be in full-bloom love again, with all its emotional ups and downs."

He shuddered. "Or not in love at all."

She put her hand on his cheek. "We will be however we were always meant to be. Let me help you now, Peter. Please."

Chapter Thirteen

He couldn't believe he was doing this.

"Here's everything," Matthew said, handing over a small kit. "You sure you know what you're doing?"

"No," Peter muttered, glaring at him for even asking the doubtful question.

"Yes, he knows what he's doing," Mary Ellen said, taking his arm and squeezing it in reassurance.

She looked radiant after her hospital stay. In fact, she glowed with health, her hospital tests and examinations turning up only right-on-the-money, positive results. His own examination had turned up the same on himself. If they'd walked into a testing program for this, they would have been snatched up as perfect.

Damn.

Mary Ellen had dubbed the chemical imbalance antidote LV-235. The letters stood for love, of course; the numbers just made it sound fancy. So she said. He could think of two hundred and thirty-five reasons not to do this. She showed more faith in his work than he did. He loved her and resented her for doing so.

He looked at Matthew, whose job depended on Peter's actions. This test, unconventional as it was, could really make or break the rest of the project. God knows,

Mary Ellen had given the committee a great setup with her crazy actions, caused by being in love. All it needed was a follow-through.

He had lost perspective the moment she promised he could make unlimited love to her. He knew he had. Temptation had overwhelmed his common sense, actually another indication of how far love had taken him off course.

Peter cleared his throat. "I must be nuts."

"Yes." Mary Ellen patted his hand. "You're in love."

They left Matthew and got in her car. As they drove away from the center, Peter said, "I don't know how I let you talk me into this."

"I used logic," she said, smiling at him.

"That's what scares me the most."

"Even though I disagree with it, I think I have more faith in your theory than you do."

"No kidding," he mumbled.

"We'll be better people for doing this," she assured him. "You'll see."

"But I don't want to be a better person," he said. "And I like you the way you are."

She laughed. "There are people who would think you were nuts just for that, my father included."

"To hell with your father." He liked the sound of that. "You're fun and exciting, Mary Ellen. Sometimes too exciting, like on Valentine's Day, but as long as I keep you away from bows and arrows or important presentations, you'll be okay."

"Ah, but if I hadn't interfered with the presentation, you would have lost the grant for sure."

"Well...maybe. I know I should have faith in my work. I *do* have faith in it." He just wished he felt it in his heart. Somehow, the closer he got to taking the antidote and really finding out whether he was right or she was, the more he felt everything would go wrong. A premonition. Scientists shouldn't have premonitions, yet he had had one today. Not a premonition of failure, either, but one of success.

His feelings were all wrapped around Mary Ellen. She would change with the antidote, if he were successful. He didn't want that. If someone had told him, when he began all this, that he would lose the love he had now, he would have walked away from the study.

No, he wouldn't have, part of his brain insisted. Without knowing what he knew now, he naively would've had no problem with the idea of losing love. *Fool,* he thought. He knew he would pay an awful price for his work.

"I don't know if I want you to do this," he said. "Let me do it alone."

"No." She was adamant. "No. I won't let you lose love without me. And you know it's perfect because it's the two of us."

"You are getting too damn logical," he muttered, cursing under his breath.

The fancy, tower condominium in Ocean City, Maryland—the neutral site they had agreed upon for their grand experiment—was a study of luxury and elegance. Its two bedrooms, sunken living room, large Jacuzzi and terrace open to the sea took Peter's breath away.

"Dammit! Did you have to get this romantic, Mary Ellen?" he asked in disgust, after the bellman left. The place had hotel amenities and ownership advantages.

"Sure. That's half the experiment. Besides, Jack's

giving it to us for free, for as long as we need it. How could I pass that up?''

"Jack?" Peter spun around to face her, while she mundanely unpacked groceries in the kitchen area. He gaped at her through the open dining area. "This is Jack's place?"

"It's not mine. Ocean City, Maryland, is nice and quiet, a family-oriented—"

"Family-oriented!" Peter exclaimed. "We're supposed to have nonstop sex in a family-oriented resort?"

Mary Ellen giggled. "Kids aren't going to run in and out of the room, Peter. I thought we would be less tempted by outside events. We're way up in the penthouse, too, away from everyone."

"But this is Jack's penthouse," Peter said, returning to the heart of the matter. "What the hell did you tell him about this?"

"Nothing more than we agreed to tell everyone except Matthew—that we're going away for a vacation. In fact, I'd only mentioned wanting a vacation when Jack offered me the place, if we didn't already have a destination yet. I thought it was perfect for what we really wanted. Relax, Peter."

"I don't like this."

"It's really sweet that you're jealous," she said.

"I'm not jealous," he said defensively. He remembered something. "You've been here before! You pulled right into the place when we first arrived."

She burst out laughing. "Peter, you read me the directions! A blind man couldn't have missed the huge Sand Dollar Condominiums marquee out front, and neither could I."

"Maybe not," he grumbled, still suspicious.

"Not maybe. Of course. Make yourself useful, it'll help. Go put the suitcases in the bedroom."

Still grumbling, he carried the two bags they'd brought into the other room. The late-afternoon shadows did nothing to hide the king-size bed, its coverlet a dramatic black-and-white satin. *Jack's place. Jack's bed.*

Peter set the suitcases down on the bed, then walked out onto the balcony. He gazed down on the blue-gray water, twenty floors below. The waves, lit an orange-pink by the setting sun behind him, thrust one after another onto the dark sand. The water pulled back, then surged forward, endlessly teasing and fulfilling.

"Even the damn ocean's having sex," Peter muttered, feeling overwhelmed by all the symbolism. Couldn't Mary Ellen have picked a broken-down shack next to a garbage dump? That worked for him.

He turned around, only to find her laying clothes from her opened suitcase onto the bed. Her suitcase was bigger than his, but he had thought that a typical woman's thing. But now she took out the sheerest black negligee he had ever seen. Granted, he wasn't an expert on negligees, but he wasn't stupid, either. The thing was a wisp of nothing.

"When I knew we would be doing the test, I went shopping at Victoria's Secret." She held the negligee up to her body. "Like it?"

Sweat broke out on Peter's forehead when he envisioned her white body encased in the material. He tried to speak, but his tongue stuck to the roof of his mouth. He nodded, the only communication he could manage.

"Good. I brought every sexy thing I could think of...."

I'm a dead man, Peter thought.

"I figure we'll know if the antidote's working when I have no interest in putting sexy things on or you have no interest in taking them off."

The latter would never happen in his lifetime, antidote or not. She lifted up a red wisp that looked like a lace teddy, only sexier, with its sheer panels on the sides rather than down the middle. *Definitely* not in his lifetime.

"That's like the chicken-and-the-egg question," she continued, shaking out the red-lace garment. "Which will happen first? Will you lose interest in taking the sexy things off me? Or will I lose interest in putting them on?"

Peter strode over and pulled the teddy thing from her hand. He tossed it over his shoulder and said, "Who cares?"

When he took her down to the bed, she protested, "But we haven't had our antidote yet."

"I know."

He made love to her so thoroughly that he forgot about romantic spots, sexy nighties and who owned the bed. Afterward, he decided the bed now knew full well who was the better man.

And it wasn't Crowley.

"INCREDIBLE," Mary Ellen murmured, kissing Peter's bare chest.

Never had he been so aggressive or wild with her. The things he'd done... She could only think what would happen when she actually put the lingerie on. Her body felt exhausted and yet totally sated already.

"Incredible," she murmured again. She was silent for a moment, then said, "We really shouldn't have done that, wonderful though it was."

Peter snorted. "But you said that's what you wanted."

She raised her head, her breasts deliciously brushing against his chest hairs. She felt the rush of heat along her veins and gulped in air to cool her body. "I know what I said, but I meant after we take the LV-235 first. Shouldn't we be taking it or something now?"

Peter rose up, setting her gently aside as he did. "I'm hungry. It's dinnertime, isn't it?"

Naked, he padded across the room. Mary Ellen admired the long, lean, muscled line of his spine and buttocks. One cheek still held his fading scar. To her bemusement, it actually looked heart shaped. It would never disappear, she thought. He would bear her mark forever.

He picked up his clothes and went into the bathroom.

Mary Ellen stared at the ceiling, remembering the fury and the poignancy of their lovemaking. She couldn't count how many times she had said "I love you" to Peter. Nor how many times he had said the same to her. Now he was cold and distant. She understood the irony. He had discovered love at the moment he discovered how to cure it.

In another twist of irony, she had to be strong for Peter. She didn't want to be, she thought, wiping a trickle of tears from her eyes. But because she loved him so much, she would sacrifice her love to this. However it turned out, she trusted that their relationship would survive this test and would be even better afterward, deeper and more abiding. She prayed he would see how much love could be missed and would give this up. This was her final chance to show him love shouldn't be tampered with.

She heard the shower running. Peter and she had

never made love in a shower yet. Maybe they could take one more time for themselves before they succumbed to necessity. Maybe…

She got up and went into the bathroom. Peter's silhouette was outlined behind the rippled-glass door. His stomach was flat, his hips narrow, more a result of absentminded eating habits than a solid exercise program. She glanced lower and smiled, then opened the shower door and slipped inside.

"I got very hungry without you," she said.

He smiled, clearly a reluctant one, but a smile nonetheless.

She took the soap from him and began to lather it up in her hands.

THE NEXT MORNING, before Mary Ellen even had to tell him, Peter knew what he had to do.

After breakfast, he stared at the kit Matthew had given him and finally opened it. The dosages had been laid out in pill form, with a nice cherry coating to make them go down easily.

He and Mary Ellen had made love again last night and this morning. So far they had yet to take a single milligram of LV-235. Peter had used the excuse that it was better to start with a full day's dosage, so that the project could be more properly charted. *What bull,* he thought. What great bull, too, because it had worked.

Mary Ellen came into the room, carrying two filled water glasses. "Okay. We've had breakfast, so we really ought to take…oh, you've got it all out."

"Yes, I got it out."

She sat next to him on the white leather sofa, setting the glasses on the coffee table before them. She said nothing while they both gazed at the kit.

Finally, after long, agonizing minutes, Peter said, "Are you sure you want to do this?"

"No, but I have to. For your sake."

"To hell with my sake!" he snapped, irritated. "You don't have a thing for Jack or anybody else, and you want a good excuse to get rid of me?"

In answer, a leather pillow whapped him hard in the mouth.

Mary Ellen whacked him again and again, the pillow punctuating her words. "How dare you! How can you even *think* I could give myself to you like that...so free, so—so intimate...and want to be with someone else? I can't believe you would even say it, you idiot!"

Somehow, from under his arms, held up to protect himself, Peter managed to say, "Hey! I'm sorry!"

She stopped the pillow bashing, but kept the mouth going. "I ought to kick you from here to Florida for thinking such a thing!"

He straightened. "I guess love's made me crazy...."

Realizing exactly what he was saying, he paused and looked at her. She stared back, stricken.

"We really are prime candidates," he said in a low voice. "I'm jealous and saying hurtful things to you."

"And I'm angry and violent with you," she admitted.

He drew in a deep breath, then pulled out their first dosage. "We have to take one every four hours."

She held up her pill. "I hope it doesn't taste as bad as the first time."

"It shouldn't. Besides, what you took was for intravenous use, not normal consumption methods. Matthew prepared it so that we would get a proper dose in an easily dispersed form."

She dropped her pill in her other palm. Peter did the same. They picked up their glasses.

"I'll always love you somewhere," Mary Ellen said, with a tiny catch in her voice. But her gaze was sure and warm, filled with confidence in what she was doing.

"I'll always love you, Mary Ellen." Peter knew it was true. No pill, nothing could totally kill what he felt for her. Not today. Not ever.

They leaned forward and kissed each other, a sweet, lingering kiss filled with their love. Then, putting their respective pills in their mouths and taking one last look, they swallowed, washing them down with the water. They were silent for a long time.

"I don't feel any different," Mary Ellen said.

He laughed. "Of course, you won't. Not yet."

"Oh."

They sat awhile longer on the sofa, then snuggled together. Peter loved the feel of her in his arms. Her body was supple, slenderly curved, her skin warm like silk. Her arms curled around his shoulders tightly. Her face was against his cheek, her hair tickling his ear. He loved that. All kinds of good feelings washed through him about her.

She was beautiful, absolutely took his breath with the way her thick, auburn hair curved around her features. Her pale pink lips enticed him to kiss them. Her creamy skin tempted him. That she was ready and willing to sacrifice her feelings to help him this way, even if it was to show him how much he might miss love, filled his heart with so much of the emotion that he thought he would burst from it.

She must have felt his gaze on her, for she turned and smiled at him. His heart really did burst with love.

The feeling was so wonderful, spreading out and filling his body completely with incredible well-being.

"I love you so much," they said at the exact same moment.

Peter laughed, happy to be alive. Happy to be with her. He would never forget this moment. Never.

He took her hands and pulled her up from the sofa. He led her into the open area of the living room and began to spin her around in a circle. Faster and faster they spun together, like little kids who'd just found a treasure trove of candy. Mary Ellen laughed delightedly. Peter laughed with her.

"Stop! Stop!" she said, still laughing. "I'm so dizzy."

Peter stopped spinning her around, but the room still spun crazily. Mary Ellen clung to him as if he were a lifeline. They staggered back to the sofa and collapsed on it.

"I feel so good," Mary Ellen said. "Is this the way the antidote works? Oh, but it can't be that, because I still love you, Peter. I feel that love for you in every bone and tissue of my body. It's so clear to me, like a living entity inside myself. I wouldn't feel like this if the LV-235 was working already."

"It shouldn't." He grinned. He just couldn't help smiling at her. In fact, his mouth felt odd. He tried to stop grinning, but his lips refused to obey. The smile widened even more. "It suppresses the chemical imbalance. Because we still feel it, especially as strongly as we do, we know it hasn't taken effect yet. It'll be a few days, I'm sure, before we see results. I should monitor our bodies, but you know what I'd rather do?"

"What?" she asked, stretching her arms above her head.

Peter reached out and began to unbutton her striped

shirt. "I'd rather see you naked against the leather of this sofa. Then I'd rather make love to you on it."

"I like the sound of this."

He stripped the shirt from her and started on the rest of her clothes. "Then I want to make love to you on every chair in the house, including the breakfast stools."

"Don't forget the top of the refrigerator."

"The top?" He eyed the object in question, visible through the open bar between the kitchen and dining area, and frowned.

She patted his cheek. "Absolutely the top. And every available floor space, too."

"Deal. But first I will worship every inch of your skin, beginning with your toes."

"Oh, boy. You're getting kinky."

"Thank you."

THREE DAYS LATER, they walked along the nearly deserted boardwalk. Only a few of the shops were open for the pre-summer foot traffic. Mary Ellen snuggled close to Peter, feeling deliriously happy.

And so in love.

"This has been just wonderful," she said. "Wasn't the desk clerk sweet this morning when he greeted us? I just love him."

"Me, too," Peter agreed. His arm was around her, and he captured her hand, intertwining her fingers with his. "I love this place, this boardwalk…"

Several people passed them, going in the opposite direction.

"…And I love those people," Peter added expansively.

Mary Ellen giggled at him. He was so relaxed, she

thought. He ought to be. They had turned into a couple of rabbits, making love whenever and wherever the mood struck them. And it had struck a lot. Maybe the antidote was taking effect, since they were having the side effect the mice had. Yet she doubted it. She loved everything and everybody, more than before. Maybe she and Peter were making up for time lost while they had hidden their relationship.

She pointed into the distance. "Look! Look at the kites!"

Huge kites flew above the beach. One, at least twenty feet long and shaped like a man, flapped in the strong ocean breeze. Under it sailed a black-and-white cow the size of a tank, its udders flopping happily high above their heads. Multicolored streamers and cornucopia spinners danced merrily along the line, which reached far into the sky.

She and Peter ran toward the kites, discovering that opposite them on the boardwalk was the shop from which they originated. The two of them watched the kites with awe until their necks hurt from continually looking up, then went into the shop together.

Kites of every imaginable color and shape hung from the ceiling. Interspersed among them were flags and wind socks, while the counter held a jumble of toys and educational puzzles.

"This is the most marvelous place I've ever been in," Mary Ellen said, spinning around and trying to look at everything at once. "I love it!"

"I love it, too," Peter said. "Let's buy a kite and fly it."

She clapped her hands. "We must."

They bought three—a fierce dragon, a rainbow sail and an old-fashioned diamond kite. Mary Ellen also bought two flags, several wind socks, and T-shirts for her and Peter that advertised the shop.

As they paid, she gazed at the store clerk, a young, good-looking man. Her heart filled with those wonderful feelings she'd been experiencing for days now.

"I love you," she told the clerk impulsively.

The clerk glanced up from the register, wide-eyed with astonishment.

Peter beamed. "Hey. I love you, too, man."

The clerk's jaw dropped.

When they were outside, Mary Ellen said, "That was so nice, Peter. You weren't jealous at all."

"I wasn't. You know, I meant it," he said. "I was just feeling so damn good after buying the kites that I wanted to share my feelings. I wanted to say it first— but you beat me to it."

"It's been three days," she commented. "If anything, I feel even more love than ever before. Is that right, Peter?"

"Hell, honey, you got me. I don't know how long it'll take for the LV-235 to kick in. We've been taking it faithfully on schedule, so I would have thought those feelings would have eased by now, but I'm not complaining."

"Me, neither." She glanced at him. "I can't wait to get home and take the next dose."

Peter juggled the packages in his arms to glance at his watch. "It's almost time, anyway. Want to skip the kite flying and go home to take our medicine?"

"Oh, absolutely." She grinned slyly. "I'll race you."

Chapter Fourteen

"Do we have to go home?" Peter asked, not wanting an answer. "Can't we stay forever?"

Mary Ellen stretched and rolled over on him. She stroked his chest. "Why did I ever think you were a workaholic?"

He grinned. "I told you I wasn't."

"We've been to the movies every night. We've rented about six this week, too. The Sunday paper is still waiting for us to read it from front to back. I really must be from the Show Me state because you've shown me."

"I thought you were born in Philadelphia."

"I was speaking metaphorically."

"Sounds kinky. So can we stay forever?"

She laughed. Her happiness shone out of her like a beacon. Peter had always thought her vibrant, but she seemed more so than ever. She said, "Why not? Who cares about work or anything? I just want to be with you. We've had so little of just being able to be together. I can't get enough."

"I want to be with you all the time." He grinned and rubbed her back, marveling at the smoothness of her skin. "God, how I love you."

"I love you so much, too."

They kissed fervently. Seven full days had passed since their arrival at the condo. Their love nest, they called it now. Peter knew he was even more in love with Mary Ellen than before. He knew he should be concerned that the antidote hadn't yet taken effect. Yet worry was the farthest thing from his mind. They should be on their way back to Philadelphia now, but he couldn't see the rush.

"So Jack won't mind if we stay longer?" he asked, just to check.

"Jack said I could have the condo for as long as I need it." She smiled. "He told me he never uses it."

"Maybe he ought to give it to us," Peter said, deadly serious. "We appreciate its beauty far more than he does. I'll talk to him about that. The man's a positive person. He'll see the positive effects of giving the condo to us."

Mary Ellen nodded. "How could he not? He's bound to understand, especially when he gets his LV-235 pills. Although, Peter, I feel I should tell you that I'm still feeling a lot of love for you. For everything, really."

"Me, too. I was just thinking that I ought to be worried that the pills haven't really taken effect yet, but maybe Matthew and I calculated the dosage too low. I can't imagine how we could have, though. We were very precise and checked the amount five times, to be absolutely sure. I wasn't taking any chances with your health again. It's just being a little slower than I expected. It's bound to take effect soon."

Only he had been saying that for a while now. And it hadn't happened yet.

"I suppose." Her amusement faded a bit, a rare occurrence for her at any time, but especially after the past week. She had been joyous. He could think of no other word to describe her. She continued, "I'm going to be very sorry when LV-235 does take effect. All this love I feel is so wonderful."

"I feel the same way," Peter admitted. "And that puts me in a dilemma. I don't want to lose these feelings. It seems…sinful to think of doing so."

"But you can't get the grant if you don't."

"I don't know," he mused. "Maybe I worry too much. Something's bound to turn up, even if the grant doesn't."

"You sound like Mr. Micawber. I think he's still waiting for that something to turn up. We'll just have to give the experiment more time."

"Oh, absolutely." He snuggled her against him, content and thrilled. A sense of having done this before stole over him. Of course, he'd done this before with Mary Ellen. But the sensation troubled him, acting like a pointer. If only he knew where it was pointing. He dismissed the troubling thoughts. The realization would come when it was good and ready. Meanwhile, he would enjoy this time with Mary Ellen.

"I think we should be married," Peter said, just as the new notion came to him.

Mary Ellen sat up. "You do?"

"Of course I do." He checked his gut. Yup, never had he meant something so strongly. "You shoot me in the butt, we get married. I know a Pavlovian reaction when I see one."

"But we had a discussion before about marriage. You had all those reasons why we weren't ready."

"What the hell do I know?" He pulled her down to

him. "Mary Ellen, will you marry me? This is the part where you say yes."

"Oh...yes."

He eyed her. "A little more enthusiasm would be appreciated."

"Ah..." She kissed his forehead, his cheeks, his lips, his shoulders. Punctuating her kisses with yeses, she kissed her way all over his body.

He sucked in his breath when she kissed a particularly intimate spot. "This is Maryland, isn't it?"

"Last time I looked."

"We can get married real fast in this state, right?"

She raised her head. "I believe so."

"Then let's get married tomorrow."

"Tomorrow?" she squeaked.

"Tomorrow," he said firmly.

Now that was a marriage proposal.

THAT EVENING, Peter took out two pills and stared at them. "These are the last ones."

"You're kidding." Mary Ellen started riffling through the kit. "That's all you packed?"

"We were supposed to go home today, remember? Matthew and I thought seven days would be enough."

"Well, it's not! I'm still totally in love with you," she exclaimed accusingly.

"And I'm totally in love with you," he said. "Maybe my theory's really a bust."

Surprisingly, the admission didn't hurt as it should have. He found himself a little grateful it hadn't.

"Your theory's not a bust!" she said, outraged. "The mice were happy as clams."

"Wrong genus grouping," he said.

"Genius or not—"

"Genus."

"Whatever…but those mice were glowing with contentment."

"Maybe. But that could have been caused by something else."

"But what?"

Peter shrugged. "That I don't know."

"But how can you show that the world's better off without love, and how can I show you what you'll miss, if we don't have enough of the antidote? I know! We should go home and get more."

"But I thought we were getting married!" Peter protested.

"We'll get the pills, then come back and get married."

"But we don't have any more pills at the center, either."

She gaped at him. "You don't?"

"We don't. I told you, I had Matthew make only enough for a week."

"We'll fix that."

She raced through the penthouse, throwing their things haphazardly into suitcases. Peter followed behind her, feeling like a bleating lamb with his further protests. But he couldn't budge Mary Ellen from the conviction that the experiment must go on.

"Showbiz was never like this," he muttered, feeling as though he was in a Marx Brothers state of perpetual confusion.

She even insisted on driving home. She headed straight to the research center and hustled him inside the deserted building to the lab. "Okay, let's make some more."

"It's not that easy," Peter said. "We have to convert

the materials from liquid to powder. And we don't have most of what we used anyway. We only had enough for the week's dosage—''

''Why the hell would you do something like that?'' she demanded.

''Because it should have had an effect within a day or two,'' he told her, outwardly calm. She was far too volatile right now. Inside, however, he felt as angry as she was, only he couldn't say at what or who. Not at Mary Ellen. Well, he was, but he wasn't, either. ''We shouldn't have needed more than a week's worth.''

''Well, now we know different.'' She began walking around the lab. ''There's got to be something...I know!''

She picked up a test tube next to the mice cage. Peter raced over and grabbed it out of her hands. ''Oh, no! This is for *mice only*. Haven't you learned that yet?''

''I'm just trying to help. Why didn't it work?''

''You ask the question of the hour.'' Peter frowned. ''This is what I get for going outside the bounds of good, quality, conventional research. I was lured by temptation, seduced by success, overwhelmed by need....''

''Peter!''

''Right, right.'' He thought for a moment. ''I'll get Matthew in here now. We need to be tested immediately.''

Mary Ellen stared at him in horror. ''I love you with every fiber of my being, Peter Holiday, but you pump my stomach again and I'll put you through the wall!''

''True love,'' Peter said. ''Where would we be without it?''

''How MANY FINGERS am I holding up?''

Mary Ellen raised her head and stared at Peter's

hand. "Forty-three."

"Mary Ellen! Be serious!"

She glared at the love of her life. He hadn't pumped her stomach. He'd simply done everything else imaginable to her. She tried to focus on his fingers. "Two. Three. I don't know. I'm so tired, Peter. I'm so tired."

"I know we've been at it all night and we're under some stress, but we have to do this," he said, sounding far too chipper for the amount of sleep he'd had. He practically jammed his fingers in her face. "Now, how many am I holding up?"

She grabbed his hand and shoved it back in his own face. "How the hell many am *I* holding up?"

"Hostility," Matthew commented, writing something down on his clipboard.

"Definitely," Peter replied.

"I just want to go to sleep!" Mary Ellen wailed, laying her head on the workbench. The mice cage sat a few feet from her. "Fellows, you have no clue how good you have it. They just take a little stick of blood from you and analyze it. But they torture humans."

"Delusional," Matthew added.

"This is not *The Secret Of N.I.M.H.*, Mary Ellen," Peter said. "These are normal tests to measure any alterations in your behavior."

"And we know I'm hostile and delusional. Can I go to sleep now? I guarantee you'll find my behavior entirely different after a few hours of being out of it. We're supposed to get married tomorrow. Today. Remember? I'd like to look good for the event." She frowned. "Or maybe you don't want to marry me anymore."

"I love you, but you're becoming very crabby. And ridiculous."

"I wish I'd never dragged you home," she said. "We could have been happily making love in Jack's bed...or on his sofa ...or the refrigerator...."

"Wow!" Matthew exclaimed.

"Mary Ellen!"

She managed a tired smile, pleased with having aggravated Peter. "Put that in your behavioral pipe and smoke it."

"The longer this takes, the longer until you *can* sleep," he threatened.

"The longer this takes, the less cooperative I'll be," she threatened back.

Peter threw up his hands in exasperation.

"Ms. Magnussen, I'm puzzled," Matthew said. "When did you first have these feelings of well-being?"

She frowned, the question capturing her wandering attentions. "I'm not sure. Maybe the second or third day we were there...no, I remember Peter laughing and spinning me around in circles the morning after we arrived at the condo." She brightened. "That was it! I'm usually a positive person, but that really was a sensational feeling."

"Why are you cooperating with Matthew and not with me?" Peter demanded.

"Because I like Matthew," she said, smiling smugly.

Peter snorted. "You just want to make me nuts."

"That, too. Besides, Matthew might let me take a nap. We know you *won't*."

"Don't be ridiculous. All you have to do is answer my questions."

"But they never end!"

"Matthew's haven't, either."

"But he's different—"

"Please," Matthew interrupted. "You're both tired."

"And crabby," she and Peter said together, then grinned reluctantly at each other.

"I wouldn't be, if I made love on the refrigerator," Matthew said enviously.

He looked at Peter with awe. Mary Ellen chuckled. She didn't have the heart to tell Matthew they'd never quite made it to the top of the refrigerator. Although there was that time...

"Did that sensational feeling occur before or after you took one of the pills?" Matthew asked.

"After," Mary Ellen said, remembering. "It was almost right after."

Matthew frowned. So did Peter.

"And that feeling continued...?"

"Well...yes, I think so. Pete and I did get wrapped up in each other. *Very* wrapped up in each other."

Matthew flushed a bright pink, clearly understanding her meaning. "You mean you had sex."

Mary Ellen looked at Peter. She smiled. "We made *love*. There's a huge difference, Matthew."

The assistant cleared his throat. "Okay. Did it feel like *love* after you started taking the pills?"

"Absolutely."

"You sure?"

"Absolutely."

"Our mice have been more active sexually—"

"Yes, I know," Mary Ellen interrupted.

"Okay. So were you and Peter...?"

Mary Ellen paused. She wondered how to answer

the question diplomatically, then decided to hell with it. "We put the mice in the shade. Wait a minute, though. We might have been responding to having the freedom of a relationship. Before the presentation, we were afraid we'd compromise the grant, so we could barely see each other and when we did we would sneak around. In Ocean City, we made love frequently before we started to take the pills."

"At the same pace as afterward?"

"I feel like my love life's on parade here," Peter grumbled.

"I feel like you're my new god," Matthew said.

Mary Ellen giggled. "It is on parade. That's the point, remember?" She turned to Matthew, feeling more alert. The kid was going somewhere with this, which meant she'd be going to sleep anytime now. "I think it was about the same pace as before the pill, but the feelings of love were stronger. I remember thinking all the time how much more I loved Peter. I remember being afraid I wouldn't when the pills finally took full effect. Most of the reason I did this was to show Peter what he would be missing without love, so I wanted him to be sure how much I did love him before we lost the feeling. At the condo, Peter told me he loved me all the time." She laughed. "We even loved the desk clerk and the people on the boardwalk and the birds and the kites and the store clerk. We nearly scared that guy to death with our love, remember, Peter? We loved everybody and everything."

"*After* taking the pills?" Matthew gasped, shocked.

"Yes. After."

"I don't understand this," he said. "I don't understand at all—"

"I've got it!" Peter suddenly shouted, leaping out

of his chair. "We had the euphoria after taking the
LV-235. The mice are happier, more loving if you will,
after taking the LV-235. We loved everything, just like
the mice. We couldn't say it enough, even, and we fed
on that. I haven't cured a chemical imbalance, I think
I've somehow found a love potion!"

"What?" Mary Ellen gasped. Wheels spun in her
mind as she thought back over their time in the condo.

"No," Matthew said.

"Look at the evidence," Peter countered. He began
to tick points off on his fingers. "We know the antidote
rebalanced the chemicals in the brain, but without al-
tering general mood like drugs would. The mice were
calmer, more contented, yet going about their normal
business. We were calmer, more contented, going
about our normal business. But the mice couldn't tell
us what they were actually *feeling*. Because they
couldn't, we had to make certain assumptions based on
their behavior. But I know how I felt on the LV-235.
We can ask how Mary Ellen felt. We both admit that
we had the exact opposite effect than expected. I don't
know how that happened, but it did."

Mary Ellen threw her arms around Peter's neck. She
kissed every inch of his face that she could reach. "Oh,
Peter, it's wonderful. Wonderful! You'll make the
world a better place just as you want, but you won't
be eliminating love. You're just taking out its down-
side. My God, you're Cupid himself! I'm so happy."

"I'm not sure how I feel," he admitted, putting an
arm around her to hold her against him. "It's confus-
ing, but I think that as long as the end result will be
the same, I'll be okay with it. My aim has always been
to stop people from hurting each other and to be more
productive."

"Maybe a little too much," she said, laughing. "You'll have to do something about the population control. Everyone will be—"

"Stop!" Matthew shouted.

Startled, Mary Ellen let go of Peter.

Matthew clenched his hair. "I can't stand this any longer! It's not a love potion. It's not anything. I gave you sugar pills."

"What?" Peter yelped the same moment she did.

"Sugar pills. Placebos. They were all placebos. I switched the stuff we made, Peter. I had to. There is no antidote."

Mary Ellen gasped. "Ar~ you telling me we had all those feelings for nothing? Not a one was real?"

"I don't know what you felt, but it wasn't from the antidote," Matthew said. "I thought I could fake my way through this again but I can't. I...dammit, I made a mistake in the early findings."

"That's impossible," Peter said. "I would have found it."

"You didn't do the actual grunt work, remember? You've left that to me for years now. Because you did, I was able to cover up the mistake, while I tried to find where it went wrong. But nothing I did corrected the problem."

"But I checked the analysis. And the controls."

"Which I put together. It was easy to hide what happened, with you leaving everything to me to do."

"I trusted you," Peter said. "Obviously that was a mistake. Show me what you did, dammit!"

Matthew ran to the shelves that held lab notebooks. He pulled out several and brought them back.

Peter flipped through them, Matthew showing him precisely where the project to eliminate automatic emotional responses, beginning with romantic love, had gone so wrong. Peter's face changed from grim to ashen. Mary Ellen knew he believed his assistant. Her heart went out to him. Peter had worked so hard on his project, hoping to help the world, and now he would have to start all over again. She didn't even feel a twinge of satisfaction that she had been right about love.

After closing the last notebook, Matthew added, "By the time I discovered what had happened, the center had moved far forward with the project. It was too late. I kept covering things up, hoping that I would find a way to dead-end it without having to confess what I'd done."

"But the mice," Mary Ellen said, thinking of something they overlooked. "They responded to the antidote. They were happy."

"The antidote is totally useless. I've had them on a light sedative to cover it up." Matthew looked at Peter. "I'm sorry, Peter. I never meant for this to happen."

"You let me apply for a grant, knowing it was based on a lie?" Peter said, his voice low. It sent a shiver of warning along Mary Ellen's spine. She knew he was furious. "Do you know how foolish the center will look when this comes out?"

"I didn't mean to, but I didn't know how to stop it," Matthew began.

"You tell me what was going on—that's how you stop it!"

"I didn't think we'd actually win the grant."

"Matthew!" Mary Ellen gasped in horror.

"Well, the other candidates have such great projects that I figured they would overwhelm ours," he defended.

"Are you working for Jeremy Chelios?" Peter asked. "Was I deliberately sabotaged? Just answer me that."

"No. Oh, no. I would never do such a thing to you. Peter, I respect you." Matthew sounded completely sincere. "It was all a stupid mistake on my part, and I would take a lie-detector test to prove it to you. I'm ruined, Peter. I know it, so lying about sabotage would be stupid at this point. I know I should have told you when it first happened, but I thought I could get it fixed. By the time it was too late for that, I thought once we lost the grant, I could get us out of this without the mess coming to anyone's attention. I thought I had a good chance of that when you two went off together with the placebos. But you should have felt *nothing* different than before. I don't know how the hell you could have felt so wonderful. It's ridiculous."

"It's not ridiculous," Mary Ellen snapped. "We're in love! Haven't you ever been so in love that you're feeling wonderful all the time? That you need to be with your love all the time? No. I can certainly tell you haven't."

"Get out, Matthew," Peter said. "Just get out."

Matthew didn't argue the point. He left quickly, probably grateful to disappear before Peter killed him. Mary Ellen had to fight the urge to do it herself. As soon as they were alone, she wrapped her arms around Peter.

He closed her tightly in his embrace, burying his face against her shoulders.

"I'm so sorry, Peter," she whispered. "I am really and truly sorry."

"How could he have done that?" he asked, raising his head.

"I don't know." She took his face in her hands and kissed him. "You can start over. Just begin where Matthew made the mistake."

He smiled wryly. "I can't believe you're the one suggesting that. You've been spending all this time trying to show me the project's wrong."

"But I want to win fair and square, Peter. What happened here wasn't fair, and I don't feel right about it." She grinned. "I'll fight the good fight with you once more. Besides, I wouldn't mind showing you what you'll miss all over again."

His smile widened. She was glad she could cheer him a little.

"Come on," she said. "Let's go home."

PETER DIDN'T TAKE a nap.

He meant to. He had lain down with Mary Ellen in his bed. They had even made love—slow languorous love that was every bit as intense as the lovemaking of the day before. Never had he needed human closeness more. Mary Ellen's closeness. Mary Ellen's love. For a little while, Matthew's betrayal almost hadn't mattered.

Mary Ellen had fallen asleep almost right away, but even though his body had been exhausted and sated, his mind still raced with the disastrous news Matthew had given them.

Other thoughts had eventually trickled in. Logical thoughts. Triggering thoughts gave him a new look at his original theories and where they'd gone wrong. He wasn't about to sleep at all after that.

He sat with his back to the headboard, a pillow propped behind him. The late-afternoon sun had spread its dark gold rays through the window by the time

Mary Ellen finally rolled over, fluttered her eyelids and yawned, coming awake.

She stretched. "My goodness, but I slept. What time is it?"

Peter glanced at his nightstand clock. "Five-thirty in the afternoon. Mary Ellen, we need to talk."

She blinked a few times, clearly trying to get the sleep from her eyes. "Okay. But I don't guarantee coherency."

"I don't think I'll ever find Nirvana by eliminating automatic emotional imbalances," he began. "We can't eliminate them. Something you said made me look at it in a whole different light."

"Me?" She sat up next to him and leaned against the headboard, holding the covers to her naked breasts.

He smiled. "Yes, you. It was when Matthew said he couldn't understand how we had any reaction while taking the placebos. That we shouldn't have had any reaction at all."

"And I said we were in love. Which we are."

He took her hand and kissed it. "We most definitely are. But Matthew was right. We shouldn't have acted any differently. But we did. We were euphoric, Mary Ellen, just by being together."

"Well, I did say earlier that we were finally free to express ourselves however we liked."

He grinned. "We certainly did. We were free to be together and we were in love. Those conditions alone were enough to make us euphoric. Now combine them with our supposed knowledge that we were taking something that would remove our love for each other. Some part of us panicked and our euphoria went off the charts."

"But it's how I feel about you."

"Exactly. The more we expressed it, the more we fed off it and the more it grew. I've thought about this all day today, looking at what went wrong with the early results and how we reacted while under the influence, so to speak. I think it's the psychological imbalance that triggers the physiological imbalance, not the reverse."

"What does that mean?" she asked.

"The emotion exists first, creating the chemical imbalance second. When I reached that conclusion, I realized that suppressing the chemical imbalance won't stop the original emotion, which is what I was trying to do. In people who have mental behavioral problems, like psychotics, we can see a definite imbalance of either brain tissue or blood enzymes and chemicals, which we treat with deadening drugs. There it's the physical that starts the mental problem. But how can you stop a state of mind with nothing concrete to latch on to?" He corrected himself. "Not a state of mind— a state of the heart. You can't stop that."

"So there's no cure for love," she said.

"Nope. You were right all along, while I had a paper tiger by the tail."

"I'm sorry," she said.

He leaned over and kissed her. "Don't be. It's funny, but I'm not that disappointed. I think because I really *have* experienced love, I understand the difference now. I couldn't before. Looking back with hindsight on every step I took, I can see the difference so clearly. I might never have seen it without you, Mary Ellen. Eventually, someone would have discovered the flaw in my findings. I would have been a laughingstock."

"Maybe Matthew actually did you a favor," she said.

"Maybe," he conceded. "I'm wondering if Matthew actually did make a mistake, after all. It might even have dead-ended, and he only thought he did something wrong."

"What will you do?" she asked.

"The first thing I'll do is to withdraw from the grant."

She gasped. "Peter, the center will be ruined."

"Better that than to lie." He smiled sadly and took her hand. "I have to. If I were to win the grant now, I'd be taking the money under false pretenses and spending the next ten years covering it up. My integrity won't let me, even without this revelation. The center will survive somehow. I'll work damn hard to find a way. And if it doesn't survive, then it was never meant to. I'll put it out that my research suddenly dead-ended. That's happened to a lot of scientists, and best of all, it wouldn't be a lie."

"My father said a great scientist makes leaps of logic to new conclusions, that it's an instinctive thing. Peter, are you sure about this?"

"I'm sure." He said it without hesitation. He knew it deep in his heart.

"I trust your instincts completely."

"Your instincts were better than mine from the beginning. Man shouldn't alter love."

She kissed him. "Peter, I'm so sorry."

"I'm not." He meant it. "It feels right to walk away. Will you go with me now to see your father? I don't know that I could get to him without you. And I'd just like for you to be there, Mary Ellen."

"Of course I'll go."

"Good." He chuckled. "When I think of us down

there in Ocean City, saying 'I love you' to everything in sight!''

She started laughing with him. "We were funny, but it was true textbook love euphoria.''

"The good part is," Peter said, "we can have that same feeling anytime we want. Because we love each other.''

Mary Ellen threw her arms around his neck. "By George, I think you've finally got it!''

They walked into her father's office several hours later. John Magnussen kissed his daughter, shook Peter's hand, then waved them into chairs. He sat on the edge of the desk and raised his eyebrows, waiting.

"I won't take much of your time, sir," Peter said. "I wish to withdraw my grant application.''

"Really?''

"Yes, sir. Recent research has shown me that the control of a chemical imbalance has dead-ended. It's impossible to achieve grant goal, therefore, with due respect, I cannot continue to vie for the grant.''

Magnussen turned to Mary Ellen. "So you didn't fall out of love with this guy?''

She smiled and shook her head. "I fell more in love with him. Never more in love than right now.''

Peter reached out and took her hand. "And I've never been more in love with your daughter than right now.''

"Does this have anything to do with the threat you mentioned at the symposium, Mary Ellen?''

"No." She smiled. "It really did dead-end, Dad.''

"This shows a lot of integrity, Peter, to come forward on the eve of a final decision.''

Peter smiled. "Thank you, sir.''

"Who do you think should get the grant?" Magnussen asked.

Peter didn't even have to think. "Bill Underwood. His work is impeccable and will benefit more people than any other."

Magnussen chuckled. "That's my choice, but don't tell anyone yet."

"I thought you liked Jeremy's frogs," Mary Ellen said.

"I toyed with the frogs. I admit it. That would have gotten a lot of press, the rain-forest destruction being a hot topic right now. So would yours, Peter. It would have been a sensation, and the grant would have given it tremendous legitimacy. Sure it's dead-ended?"

"Positive," Peter said firmly.

"Too bad. But Bill's third-world research will be the greatest benefit to the most people. I couldn't say no to it, and I don't intend to."

"One more thing," Peter said. "Mary Ellen and I are getting married." He turned to her. "We are getting married, aren't we?"

She smiled and squeezed his hand. "Oh, Peter."

He turned back to her father. "That's a yes."

"I see." Magnussen looked amused.

"We were supposed to get married today in Maryland, but everything's probably closed now."

"Tomorrow, then," Mary Ellen said.

"Now hold on a damn minute." Magnussen said thunderously. "You're my only child, and I'm not letting you get married without a big bash. You two have to have a church wedding at the Saints Peter and Paul Basilica and a reception at the Warwick. I want to show off my son-in-law, the scientist. You couldn't have shot

Linda Cajio 247

a better guy in the rear, Mary Ellen, and I want the world to know it.''

Peter looked at Mary Ellen. She looked back at him. They burst into laughter together.

A short time later, when they were standing on the sidewalk, Peter put his arm around her and said, ''Well, that's that. Want to come with me to the lab and help me destroy my notes? There's no sense keeping them now.''

''I'd be honored,'' Mary Ellen said. ''How do you feel knowing we'll have to suffer through love like the rest of the poor slobs in the world?''

''It'll be all the sweeter because we'll find our own way through it,'' he said. ''For the rest of our lives.''

''Until death do us part, God help us,'' she intoned. ''Good or bad, love will have to find its own way. Hey, that's logical! Who says I can't be logical?''

''Not me,'' Peter answered.

He kissed her. With love.

Epilogue

"You may kiss the bride."

The bride had never looked more radiant, Peter thought. Not even when they had been in the "grip" of LV-235. An old-fashioned lace veil hid Mary Ellen's rich auburn hair, but her eyes sparkled crystal blue and her creamy skin matched porcelain. Her gown clung to her form, its high choker neck modest. The back, however, was completely sheer from shoulder to a scant, shocking inch above the sensual dimples at the curve of her derriere. Only an endless row of buttons along her entire spine hid any flesh. Peter wondered how he would get them all undone, then decided to worry about it later.

He gave Mary Ellen Holiday the first in a lifetime of kisses. His father had been wrong about a marriage without love. Intimate friendship was all wrapped up in the emotions, but man needed love. Peter knew *he* needed love.

In the reception line afterward, he introduced her to all the relatives she hadn't yet met, privately pleased they had come out in force for his wedding. He was having a grand time. He never knew weddings could actually be so much fun. Maybe that was because he was finally and truly in love.

His three cousins gathered off to the side of the church steps and shook hands among themselves. The men were all around Peter's age and looked enough like him to claim relations.

"I hear your law practice is doing well," Michael Holiday said to his cousin, Jared Holiday.

"Trying," Jared replied, grinning at his cousin. "Your columns are in every newspaper I pick up."

Michael laughed. "I wish."

"Do you believe this?" Raymond, the city's hottest radio sports-show host, asked. He was the fourth Holiday cousin. "Who the hell would have thought Peter would take the plunge?"

"Not me," Michael admitted, chuckling.

"He always talked about getting rid of love, didn't he?" Jared commented.

Raymond snorted. "That was Peter. Nuts."

"Nah. Just innocent," Michael said. "He always has been. Now me, I know love wreaks havoc with a man's life, so I've always avoided it like the plague."

"It's love at first sight that gets me," Jared said. "I've handled more divorces caused by love at first sight. Usually the husband or wife falls in love at first sight with the secretary or the mailman."

The three laughed.

"Love," Raymond said in disgust. "Who needs it? I know I don't. But I'll admit Mary Ellen's stunning. Peter couldn't have done better. His wife's old man sure did throw a ritzy bash."

"Funny thing about that," Jared said. "Peter called me to draw up a prenuptial for them, cutting him completely out of her money."

"You're kidding!"

Jared shook his head. "Mary Ellen refused to sign it. I believe she called him an idiot of the first water."

In the reception line, Peter accepted Jack Crowley's hearty handshake. He could accept Jack—as long as the guy stayed away from Mary Ellen. Peter was back in possessive form and liking it.

"When you two get back from your honeymoon, I want to sit down with you, Peter," Jack said. "Keycast Communications and I want you to do a big, long-term study for us about fan behavior so we can predict future trends in sports. We want to be on the cutting edge for years to come."

Peter gaped, the implications swirling madly in his head.

Jack leaned forward and added, "I'll throw you another wedding present. Keycast has big money to spend on this. *Big* money."

"I love you, man," Peter said, enthusiastically pumping Jack's hand.

Jack tilted back his head and laughed. "Woohah! You feel great!"

Peter looked on happily when Jack enfolded Mary Ellen in a big bear hug and kissed her soundly.

A few moments later, she leaned over to Peter and said, "You didn't actually make a love potion when I wasn't looking, did you?"

"Not me," Peter assured her. "I've sworn off meddling with love, except for you. I love you with all my heart."

She squeezed his head. "I love you with all mine, so Cupid will have to do without you, thank goodness. He shot you in the behind with the arrow and that's enough."

"*You* shot me with the arrow, and it was enough for me," Peter said fervently. "I've learned my lesson."

Mary Ellen smiled. "Good boy. Ah, here we go...Peter, meet my great-aunt Edna...."

High above in the heavens, a cherub peeked over the edge of a fluffy little cloud and watched Mary Ellen and Peter eventually run down the church steps amid a hail of birdseed. Birdseed, rice...the couple didn't need any fertility symbol. They would be happily making babies for years to come.

Young Matthew had done his work well in foiling Peter's goal to eliminate love. If Matthew hadn't, there would have been hell to pay. Cupid smiled. He had a rep to maintain, and innocent undercover plants like Matthew ensured that. Love was safe once again.

After the newlyweds got in the black limousine, the cherub straightened. He shook out his tiny wings, then slung his bow over his shoulder. He dusted off his pudgy little hands with satisfaction.

"That'll teach him to mess with the master!"

Now that Peter was down and out, he looked at the other three Holiday men. Their time was coming. Cupid couldn't wait.

Is it better to know who you *are*...or
who you are *not*?

SECRET SINS

Twenty-seven years ago on a cold and snowy night in
Cleveland a traffic pileup leaves at least four people dead.
One little girl survives. Though she calls herself Liliana, she
is proven to be Jessica Marie Pazmany—and her parents are
among the dead. The toddler is soon adopted and becomes
Jessica Marie Zajak.

Now her well-adjusted life quickly comes to a halt when
it is discovered that the little girl in the accident could not
possibly have been Jessica Marie Pazmany—because *she* died
seven months *before* the car crash. So who is Jessica? Who
was Liliana?

The next bestseller by internationally celebrated author

JASMINE CRESSWELL

Available in February 1997 at your favorite retail outlet.

MIRA The brightest star in women's fiction

Once upon a time...

We were little girls dreaming of
handsome princes on white chargers...of
fairy godmothers who'd made us into beautiful
princesses...and of mountain castles where
we'd live happily ever after.

Now that we're all grown up,
Harlequin American Romance lets us
recapture those dreams in a brand-new
miniseries aimed at the little girl who still
lives on inside of us. Join us for stories
based on some of the world's best-loved
fairy tales in

Once Upon a Kiss...

Watch for these wonderful
fairy-tale romances, starting with

**THE PRINCE, THE LADY &
THE TOWER**
By Muriel Jensen
Available in March

Once Upon a Kiss... At the heart
of every little girl's dream...and every
woman's fantasy...

Look us up on-line at: http://www.romance.net

FAIRY 1

LOVE *or* MONEY?
Why not Love *and* Money!
After all, millionaires
need love, too!

How to Marry a
MILLIONAIRE

Suzanne Forster,
Muriel Jensen
and
Judith Arnold

bring you three original stories
about finding that one-in-a million man!

Harlequin also brings you
a million-dollar sweepstakes—enter
for your chance to win a fortune!

FREE VALENTINE'S BROOCH!
$9.95 U.S. retail value

This Valentine's Day Harlequin brings you all the essentials—romance, chocolate and jewelry—in:

VALENTINE *Delights*

Matchmaking chocolate-shop owner Papa Valentine dispenses sinful desserts, mouth-watering chocolates…and advice to the lovelorn, in this collection of three delightfully romantic stories by Meryl Sawyer, Kate Hoffmann and Gina Wilkins.

As our special Valentine's Day gift to you, each copy of *Valentine Delights* will have a beautiful, filigreed, heart-shaped brooch attached to the cover.

Make this your most delicious Valentine's Day ever with *Valentine Delights!*

Available in February wherever Harlequin books are sold.

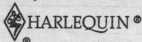

HARLEQUIN ®

Look us up on-line at: http://www.romance.net

VAL97

HARLEQUIN®

Don't miss these Harlequin favorites by some of our most
distinguished authors!
And now, you can receive a discount by ordering two or more titles!

HT#25645	THREE GROOMS AND A WIFE by JoAnn Ross	$3.25 U.S. $3.75 CAN.	☐
HT#25647	NOT THIS GUY by Glenda Sanders	$3.25 U.S. $3.75 CAN.	☐
HP#11725	THE WRONG KIND OF WIFE by Roberta Leigh	$3.25 U.S. $3.75 CAN.	☐
HP#11755	TIGER EYES by Robyn Donald	$3.25 U.S. $3.75 CAN.	☐
HR#03416	A WIFE IN WAITING by Jessica Steele	$3.25 U.S. $3.75 CAN.	☐
HR#03419	KIT AND THE COWBOY by Rebecca Winters	$3.25 U.S. $3.75 CAN.	☐
HS#70622	KIM & THE COWBOY by Margot Dalton	$3.50 U.S. $3.99 CAN.	☐
HS#70642	MONDAY'S CHILD by Janice Kaiser	$3.75 U.S. $4.25 CAN.	☐
HI#22342	BABY VS. THE BAR by M.J. Rodgers	$3.50 U.S. $3.99 CAN.	☐
HI#22382	SEE ME IN YOUR DREAMS by Patricia Rosemoor	$3.75 U.S. $4.25 CAN.	☐
HAR#16538	KISSED BY THE SEA by Rebecca Flanders	$3.50 U.S. $3.99 CAN.	☐
HAR#16603	MOMMY ON BOARD by Muriel Jensen	$3.50 U.S. $3.99 CAN.	☐
HH#28885	DESERT ROGUE by Erine Yorke	$4.50 U.S. $4.99 CAN.	☐
HH#28911	THE NORMAN'S HEART by Margaret Moore	$4.50 U.S. $4.99 CAN.	☐

(limited quantities available on certain titles)

	AMOUNT	$
DEDUCT:	10% DISCOUNT FOR 2+ BOOKS	$
ADD:	POSTAGE & HANDLING	$
	($1.00 for one book, 50¢ for each additional)	
	APPLICABLE TAXES*	$_____
	TOTAL PAYABLE	$_____
	(check or money order—please do not send cash)	

To order, complete this form and send it, along with a check or money order for the
total above, payable to Harlequin Books, to: **In the U.S.:** 3010 Walden Avenue,
P.O. Box 9047, Buffalo, NY 14269-9047; **In Canada:** P.O. Box 613, Fort Erie, Ontario,
L2A 5X3.

Name: _____

Address: _____ City: _____

State/Prov.: _____ Zip/Postal Code: _____

*New York residents remit applicable sales taxes.
Canadian residents remit applicable GST and provincial taxes.
Look us up on-line at: http://www.romance.net

HBACK-JM4